# The Mafia Leader's Cookbook

## A Novel

By

S. R. Palumbo

**ISBN: 1-4107-9612-4 (e-book)**
**ISBN: 1-4107-9611-6 (Paperback)**

**Library of Congress Control Number: 2003097924**

**This book is printed on acid free paper.**

**Printed in the United States of America**
**Bloomington, IN**

1stBooks - rev. 03/10/04

To
Dr. Mastro—
I may be haunting you
for a good while longer!
Sal Palumbo

*For David and Nicole*

(Picture on rear Cover
—me at 28!)

# 1

**In a well-orchestrated maneuver of stealth and native cunning, the leading members of the New York Mafia crime families had mingled in with legitimate mourners and steered their way to a catacombed basement of the Mattarazza Funeral Home, as umber colored and deadly grim as the enigmatic, rockbound face of its patriarch, Don Vincenzo Mattarazza, the *Cappo di Tutti Capi*, who greeted them in earnest embrace and who brightened only briefly for a moment while pointing to a newly presented, personally signed photograph of Frank Sinatra, framed on the wall between two other photos of Jesus Christ and Joe Dimaggio.**

**Don Vincenzo's well-groomed *soldati* escorted them to prearranged seats at the conference table and some pretense was consciously made at light-hearted chatter and pleasantries, but nobody seemed to be fooled by it. There was something very heavy in the air and everyone kept their eyes on each other as Don Vincenzo finally called the meeting to order, slipping into his**

**well-known "Age of Reason" look; that calm, deliberate, high-toned aura of seriousness in which all that he was—and all that he had become to them—would filter down through the darkness of his studied gaze while scanning the room and lightly playing the keyboard of the conference table with practiced hands.**

**"This is not the kind of meeting that I look forward to, but business is business. You all know the story. We gotta get rid of Big Al Gavona in South America, that no good, lowdown, dirty piece of fucking shit! We gotta make the hit on him."**

**The men at the table stirred anxiously as someone came in with a pot of coffee and placed it on an elegant tray with demitasse cups. There was Louie "The Loud Mouth" Lallo, from Queens; Patty "Balls" Auriello, from Brooklyn; Vinny "The Fixer" De Nardo, from the Bronx; and Bart "The Monster" Virgilio, from Staten Island. They agreed on the basic premise involved in making the hit, but all of them seemed to have reservations, all of which (in the words of Lallo) really boiled down to one sure thing:**

**"Who the fuck would be *crazy* enough to make a hit that would end up by being suicide? I mean…no disrespect intended, Don Vincenzo, but the whole world knows that Big Al lives on a private island in Rio de Janeiro that's so heavily guarded, he's got his own goddamn army down there. If you're lucky enough to get in there in the first place, and then make the hit…you die yourself! So who would take on a job like that?"**

**Murmurs of recognition and assent were voiced by the others, and Don Vincenzo calmly responded by shaking them with the two magic words:**

***"Nunzio Zangara."***

**"The Abruzzi Strangler?"**

**"I thought he was dead?"**

**"No, he's dying of cancer. I spoke to him the other day and told him what the whole deal was, and he said that he would do it for me...not just for the money. He does it out of respect for me."**

**The others balked at the logic of this with upturned eyes. The Strangler at the height of his fame was someone to be reckoned with, but if it was true that the man was dying, what were the guarantees involved?**

**Lallo mulled this over a moment.**

**"I understand what you're getting at, Don...he's dying, so he figures he's got nothing to lose by risking his life on a suicide mission, *va bene,* true, but if the guy is so far gone that he can't do the job—and they find out that we sent him down there?"**

**"That's a gamble that we all have to take." Don Vincenzo leveled meaningfully. He did not believe in violence for the sake of violence, nor was he disposed to wanton displays of unbridled power as a means of intimidation or repression. That was for the schifoso out there who didn't know which end was up. He was much too much a student of history to ever be swayed by such obviousness in the use of force, and realized that just the threat of it (and the awesome nature of the beast itself) had the sobering**

**psychological effect of keeping the natives from getting restless, and this is what had earned his stripes and respect throughout the underworld.**

**At sixty, he had been through the wars and had always managed to keep the peace at a reasonable price in the realm of an unreasoning profession. The call for anyone's death, therefore, was a matter of the gravest concern and never one that Don Vincenzo had ever abused or taken lightly.**

**"We gambled before by getting the Chinks to take over all our drug operation, and not for any moral reasons." Don Vincenzo reminded them. No one gave up that kind of money willingly or for passing fair. The question was one of pure survival: get out of drugs or run the risk of annihilation. The Feds were out to lop off their heads and had focused on the world renowned leaders of the New York families, one of whom had been recently arrested for "nodding" at an old friend of his who happened to be tailed at the time by narcotics agents looking for a deal to go down, and the nod was construed as a signal for the "go-ahead" in resolving the deal, for which Jimmy "The Jap" Bazilio (whose only crime was in saying "hello") was sentenced to fifteen years in the can for conspiring, not to mention the fact that the Blacks and Hispanics were killing each other—and killing cops—and getting twelve year old kids involved in selling and dealing, and all of a sudden what started out as pushover money had now become known as a crime on humanity.**

**Don Vincenzo poured out cups of demitasse and graciously rose to pass them around.**

**"And now that the Chinks have their own connections and get their supplies from the Far East and Asia, and not South America, Big Al thinks that we cut him out and made a deal, and that I'm the one who's behind all this. Not you, Mr. Lallo, and nobody else here," he underscored, "which is why he tried to whack me out two weeks ago!"**

**Had a waiter not made the fatal, but convenient, mistake of crossing into the line of fire as Don Vincenzo signaled to him for more antipasto, their meeting today would not be in the basement of the funeral home, but upstairs with the rest of the mourners.**

**Lallo took his cue from this: "We appreciate your position, Don…the sonofabitch has got to die, no doubt about it, but how you gonna get to him? I mean, Big Al never goes anywhere, he's always in hiding, and nobody gets to that armed fortress of an island he lives on unless they got a calling card."**

**"And that's exactly what they're gonna get," Don Vincenzo voiced triumphantly. "My cookbook!"**

**"What?"**

**"You heard what I said, *my cookbook* that he's been dying to get his fat little hands on all these years."**

**Auriello from Brooklyn was outraged by this.**

**"I know you over 30 years, and my wife even begged and pleaded with you, and you wouldn't give us the recipe to your**

Risotto Milanese...and now you're giving this fat tub of shit the whole fucking book?"

"Hey, Patty." Don Vincenzo stared in disbelief. "Don't you understand what I'm talking about? I use it for bait! It's the calling card we're looking for. The Strangler pretends he's defecting from me, and to show good faith he offers the cookbook with all my secret recipes in it."

Don Vincenzo explained the plan in elaborate detail and nobody murmured or said a word until Lallo shook his head again.

"How come we gotta do this ourselves and take all the chances and end up with all the dirty work?"

"And who's gonna do it, if we don't do it?"

"The fucking Chinks! It's all because of them we're in trouble for going straight."

"Yeah, we'll give a fucking Italian cookbook to someone from China, and Big Al will really go for it, right? He won't get suspicious."

A round of laughter broke the ice and Lallo retreated sheepishly.

"All right, you're right, we're over a barrel. I guess there's no other way around it, but what about Tony Stabile from Chicago? He used to be very friendly with Al."

"We all were friendly!" Don Vincenzo presented his hands as though he were weighing two outspread platters of good and evil.

**"That's why they put it in the fucking bible—if your left hand offends you, cut it off!"**

**"So whatta we do if Chicago don't go along with the hit?"**

**"Chicago will do what's good for Chicago. Tony Stabile is a mortefame. He blows with the wind."**

**"Then why don't we fucking blow him away?" Virgilio shouted. "I can't stand that fucking toothpick in his mouth."**

**"Forget Stabile." Don Vincenzo tempered cautiously. "In our kind of business we can't afford to be looking like we kill each other like animals. This ain't no fucking butcher's convention."**

**This drew a long, self-conscious lull of turgid reflection from everyone who was seated at the table.**

**"Any objections to making the hit on Big Al Gavona?"**

**No objections. Everyone grunted unanimously and rose to leave, except for Lallo, who eased his way to the head of the table, fumbling out a cigarette and making sure all the others had gone before engaging Don Vincenzo eyeball to eyeball.**

**"Just one more thing."**

**"What is it?" Don Vincenzo asked.**

**Lallo lingered hesitantly, then reached inside the pocket of his jacket—and just as quickly, one of Don Vincenzo's soldati slipped out a gun and held it with his hand on the trigger inside his coat.**

**"My family has been bugging me now for over a year, so I guess I gotta tell you about this sooner or later." He pulled out a lighter and nervously lit up his cigarette. "Can you do me a favor**

**and get me a personal, autographed picture of Frank Sinatra with all the names of my kids on it?"**

∞∞

**It was settled then. Don Vincenzo returned to his home in New Jersey (no less equipped than Big Al's place, with his own humble army of armed guards and watchdogs and the latest in surveillance technology) and immediately set his plan into action. No time wasted. Calls were made. Contacts in Brazil consulted. He also summoned his only daughter, Josephine, who had more brains in her little pinky than all his *chidroola* sons put together.**

**The only bad part, unfortunately, was the way she looked. He was never one to fool himself when it came to his children. You fool yourself there, you start to fool yourself everywhere, and the truth was that she was homely looking, physically unattractive to men, and thin as a rail. She was also headstrong and obstinate, and had driven him so insane with notes from all her teachers that finally he had been forced to violate family tradition and send her to college, which caused even deeper resentment with his sons since none of them had gotten through high school, especially Carmine, his oldest son—that Mongolian idiot!**

**Where were the Michael Corleones of this world, like the Godfather movie with Al Pacino? What would he not have given in ransom for a son like that?**

**But Josephine was as smart as a whip and could outthink any man around, if only she knew how to cook a little and didn't wear all those baggy clothes that made her look like a fucking concentration camp victim.**

**"Josephine, when was the last time you ate?" he would badger her. "How come you stopped seeing Al Vialonga? He's gonna be big in the Organization."**

**"I told you, father, I know you mean well, but I don't want you fixing me up with people who look like they were conceived in oil."**

**And always with that smirk on her face as though something about their being together or talking together was very funny and promised to get even funnier, and *nobody* laughed at Don Vincenzo, *Porco Diávolo!* God only knows what was going on in that mind of hers to get him all upset this way, and defy him this way, when he needed her more than ever right now, and this is the way she kept him waiting.**

**"Carmine, did you tell your sister I sent for her?"**

**"Yeah, I told her."**

**"Well, go tell her again."**

**"I don't like being a messenger, Pa."**

**"Why, it's too hard for you?"**

**"You know what I mean. I just don't get along with her."**

**"We all get along, this is all in the family, so go get your sister before your brain starts to shrink on you."**

∞∞

Carmine stalked to his sister's room at the rear of the house where he found her cleaning the barrel of her gun and watching an old-time video classic of Random Harvest, brushing away a tear from her eye when Ronald Coleman got hit by a car and didn't know what world he was in, while his unsuspecting, newly wed wife was waiting for him by the garden gate with "victim" written all over her face.

"How can you even watch that shit!" he yelled at her. "No wonder you ain't got no fucking boyfriends."

"Just go take a walk and mind your own business."

"You know Papa don't like guns in the house."

"This is not the house, this is where I live, and I do whatever I want to do."

"Well, the old man is waiting."

"Don't give me orders."

"They ain't any orders."

Josephine took her own sweet time, cursed silently at the stupid Greer Garson for having to wait for anyone who was dumb enough to get hit by a car while crossing the street, and leisurely sauntered down to the basement which Don Vincenzo had turned into a shrine for her mother, Consalada, replete with statues and candelabra and bulletproof walls.

"What is it?" she snapped.

"You don't say *hello*?" her father asked.

**"We saw each other this morning," she said. "What's the 'hello' bullshit?"**

**"Watch your language!"**

**Don Vincenzo, seated behind a giant size desk that looked like one of his doors had collapsed, drew in his arms to control himself. She was baiting him. She had entered the room with some rag on her head that only the fucking homeless wore.**

**"What is that?" he said. "Did you hurt your head?"**

**"It's a turban."**

**"Jesus—take it off when you're in this house. You look like my goddamn cleaning woman."**

**Josephine looked down her nose at him and jiggled out of the turban with a smirk on her face.**

**"Is this better?"**

**"Yeah."**

**She let down her hair.**

**"Papa..."**

**"What?"**

**"I said *Papa*."**

**"Ah..." The "Papa" part always got to him, the sonofabitch. She knew every little weak spot of his and also knew how to push the buttons.**

**"You see the way you upset me?" he said.**

**"Is there something important you want to discuss?"**

**He came down with his fists on the desk, and one of his upper bridges grew loose.**

"Everything I discuss is important."

"Oh, Papa, please, stop being so goddamned serious."

"You curse at me?"

She had been through this kind of scene before and inadvertently turned to the shrine with candles burning everywhere and her mother's picture plastered on a wall full of saints in a cockeyed Woppo Disney World of memoriums.

"Is this going to be an argument now?"

"I don't like the way you talk to your father."

"I'm sorry," she said. "I apologize. It's that time of month."

"Stop talking about these times of month!" Don Vincenzo exploded. "You know I don't like to hear that talk." She loved to get underneath his skin and ruffle his feathers, and Don Vincenzo would bluster and blush and fall into every trap of hers, despite himself. "I want you and Carmine to go down to Rio and oversee the entire operation."

"Carmine and I don't get along. We're from two different worlds."

"Your brother needs help. You know that he's mentally handicapped."

"Why, just because he thinks Massachusetts's a city in Boston?"

"Don't be funny!"

She purposely lit up a cigarette to watch him flinch. He hated smoke. He never drank. His only vice was in parasitically cashing in on the weakness of others, a way of life only slightly less hypocritical than big-time religion or the stock exchange, but which all moral forces had helped to define as Organized Crime—or the Mafia.

"I thought that your most trusted friend, the Abruzzi Strangler, works alone?"

"I don't trust nobody, you know that, but with Nunzio there is some concern because he has these blackout spells, he's epileptic, on top of which he's terminally ill...and this job is very complicated. I need you there to establish contact, to see to it that he's able to do what he has to do."

"You want me to make a medical decision about somebody's physical competency in a matter I know nothing about?"

You look at his hands. If his fingers are moving, the job is on. If not, we call the whole thing off and try something else."

"I never even met this man."

"And nobody who has ever met him, lived long enough to remember him." Don Vincenzo cracked.

"I know," she sneered, "But I wouldn't go around bragging about it."

"Just watch your mouth."

"I say whatever I want to say," she fired back. "Does he speak any English?"

"Of course, he speaks English! You think I send you down there with an interpreter?"

"Well, knowing Carmine..."

**"No...No...No...the man is from Brooklyn, same as us. He came here when he was ten years old."**

**"I thought you said he lived in Abruzzi?"**

**"Well, that's where they deported him when he got in trouble with the Postal Service."**

**Josephine looked aghast at him.**

**"Is he the one who attempted to mail a dismembered body to someone in the Bronx?"**

**"He never knew what was in that box!" Don Vincenzo protested. "He was framed by his cousin in the postal service who was jealous of him because of some sort of thing with a woman, but they couldn't prove a goddamn thing, so they got him on the Alien Act."**

**"The Alien Act?" she rolled her eyes disdainfully. "They should have got him for retardation. What the hell did he think he was mailing, Frozen Fish?"**

**"You call me a liar?"**

**"I don't even want to talk about it. Just tell me what you want me to do, and let's get this whole thing over with."**

**Don Vincenzo lowered his head and knelt by the light of two votive candles and crossed himself. Whenever she had him dead to rights and cornered this way, he would automatically go into his bullshit-paisano-religious routine and grovel before the foot of the shrine with outstretched arms.**

**"What're you doing?" Josephine baited. "Praying for rain?"**

"I pray to the soul of your mother for guidance, La Sacra Mama, the Saint of Saints!"

"She was also a pretty good kitchen scully."

"You shut uppa you mouth! I'm warning you." He shouted with his fist in the air and lost all semblance of any poise, along with all his painstaking efforts to never lapse into greaseball talk. "You skating on a tin a ice."

"Why, you going to put out a contract on me?"

"The devil is in you, *Porco de Miseria*! What you need is a man who can beat some kind of sense into you. Make a woman of you."

To preserve herself (and to keep from laughing right in his face), she flung out her arms in open defiance and did a little fade-away step, the old soft shoe, the buck and wing (with a little bump and grind mixed in), and such was the shock of this unexpected mocking display of wantonness—this *Mulanyana* minstrel show she was putting on—that to Don Vincenzo's utter amazement, the room began to heave and dissolve and slide away...and Josephine's face grew darker and darker...

"Whatta you doing? Stop that dancing..."

Don Vincenzo stuttered and blinked and looked up again to see if maybe his eyes were playing tricks on him. Was he losing his mind? Had they put the evil eye on him? His only daughter...*que beddu fighiu e mascalzone*...she looked like a nigger!

Josephine cut to a vengeful bow and walked to the door.

**"Is there anything else you want to discuss?"**

**But Don Vincenzo had never before lost control like this and couldn't speak.**

**"Is there anything else?"**

**"All right! Okay—I'm trying to think."**

**While her father was thinking and trying to figure out why he had been cursed this way (had he not contributed eight thousand dollars to the local parish charity drive and Knights of Columbus?), Josephine firmly resolved to leave and get out from under. This was the last of her guilt trips for him. Enough was enough! She had bought a condo on Central Park West and would simply have to melt away and disappear and try to find work where nobody knew her. Maybe even change her name and make a whole clean sweep of it, make a move for herself, a life for herself, or go down forever as Don Vincenzo's "sainted" daughter: the one who had dared to wear pantyhose while having to wear the balls in the family.**

**"Where is he staying, this friend of yours? At what hotel?"**

**"You do this for me?" Don Vincenzo choked. "You go down there?"**

**"Where is he staying?"**

**"The hotel *La Condessa del Mar*. He leaves today."**

**"I'll be there, don't worry. I'll make the trip. Who else have you got as your right-hand man?"**

**He dwelt on that as she left the room and waved a sloppy goodbye at him, though deep inside he pictured himself and**

**Josephine as he saw in all those "reunion" movies of father and child who were either on the outs with each other or separated, and always toward the end of the movie, floating across an endless expanse of flowering meadows and running to embrace each other tearfully, as though everything that had set them apart had only existed in order to have them kiss and make up and forgive each other—those lying bastards! How could they fall for shit like that?**

**After half an hour of prayerful observance, disturbed by what he had seen in his daughter and not knowing how his eyes had played such tricks on him, his mind opened up to another form of giddiness that threatened to do the same thing again, so he tried to struggle up to his feet from a kneeling position and pitched over sideways, grasping onto the leg of a chair and cursing at all this idiocy, at the impotence of the way he was acting. Thinking that maybe the end had come as he crawled and fumed to the head of the shrine where the portrait of his dearly beloved Consalada loomed overhead in an awesome frieze of perpetual anger and condemnation, her huge crooked nose swooping down at him unmercifully and resonating throughout the room like a sword thrust to the base of the spine.**

**When Carmine came in, his father was on the floor by the desk and babbling incoherently.**

**"Papa, Jesus—what the hell happened?" Carmine rushed to his side at once. "Did you hurt yourself?"**

**"...don't tell no one..." The old man grabbed at Carmine's throat. "...don't want no one to know about it..."**

**"Know about what? What's wrong with you?" But Don Vincenzo had given the sign of *Omerta* and refused to talk unless Carmine swore and pledged himself to secrecy.**

**"Okay," he said, and tried to release the stranglehold that was crushing his neck. "What is it that you don't want no one to know about?"**

**His father gagged and solemnly searched the room for spies.**

**"I think that maybe your sister is...Jewish..."**

ꝏꝏ

# 2

**The charter flight to Rio de Janeiro was due to take off in exactly two hours from Kennedy Airport, and Marvin Kopfelman, wedged in between a closet door and the radiator, was still in the process of packing his luggage and struggling with the deadly thrust of his mother's inquisitorial tone and close pursuit as she followed him through their *ongepotchket* basement apartment on Ocean Parkway, hounding him from room to room, wherever he turned or didn't turn—like a well-meaning and beneficent avenging angel.**

**"Mother, please, would you give me some room to breathe over here? You're crushing my back."**

**The room they were in was claustrophobic, and Kopfelman's mother would not relinquish another square inch of space to him.**

**"So now you're giving orders already?" she nodded sagely, hunching her back and twisting herself into martyred positions that crippled up her entire body as though from years of slaving away and sacrifice. "All you do is ask them a question, and this is**

**the kind of answer you get? That they need more room? That already they can't wait to get away?"**

**Her voice could be heard from across the street, and all she needed was one octave more and a musical score by Irving Berlin to send him into total shock.**

**"Mother, there is nobody here but us chickens," he said. "We are standing in the same room together. Why are you speaking so loud to me?"**

**"That's the way I talk."**

**"You're shouting at me like I'm deaf and dumb."**

**"Why, you think I don't know what's going on with this trip you're taking?"**

**"Why, what's going on?" he challenged her. If it wasn't the usual guilt trip they had sent him on for thirty-nine years, then already it was a threat to her beyond comprehension, and Kopfelman was not about to invoke the ghosts of the past nor unleash the demons of Sigmund Freud on so unsuspecting an audience. What he did, instead, was try to reverse the flow involved. Perfect, if he could, his backhand swing. "Do you realize that in all these years, the only place I've ever gone to is Florida?"**

**"So where else should we go in retirement?"**

**"That I never went to my high school prom…"**

**"So nobody wanted to go with you."**

**"…and that all my life, I have never done one single thing to give myself pleasure?"**

"So I have pleasure?" his mother lashed out indignantly. She had shifted now to topspin stuff with plenty of forearm, scrunching together the folds of her house robe and pounding her chest and soon exhorting the light fixture and the rest of the room for moral support and corroboration. "You think I do things to give myself pleasure?"

"Mother, will you please calm down? This is not a production of People's Court, so don't get excited."

"I'm not excited! Who's excited? All I'm doing is asking questions—and look at the way he talks to me." She turned to the bureau and chest of drawers and the art posters that she failed to comprehend at all and viewed as potential enemies. "I know," she said. "I know", she repeated. "You can't wait to get away from here."

"It's not a matter of getting away. I'm not escaping."

"Is that why you borrowed my brother's tuxedo to go on vacation?"

"I told you before, it's not a vacation."

"So how come you have to get fancy dress?"

"Your brother's tuxedo is not fancy dress, it's older than I am, fits like a tent, and has World War II lapels on it from the big band era," Kopfelman wearily rubbed his head, "but at some point in the teacher's convention, there's going to be a formal affair, and I can't afford to go splashing money on evening clothes."

"Uncle Murray said you shouldn't get any stains on it."

"I'm surprised he didn't ask for a deposit."

"It's not so funny to laugh at people who can't lose weight."

"What does weight have to do with it?"

"Just don't be such a big shot when it comes to my family."

"Your family? What're you talking about? It's my family too."

"That's right," she said, "and don't you forget it!"

Kopfelman felt a creeping sensation of instant angst that spread from his crotch to his abdomen.

"In China, this could never happen."

"What're you mumbling? What kind' affair you talking about?"

The United Federation of Teachers...dinner...dancing...who knows? Maybe I'll meet somebody."

Kopfelman's mother pulled out a sponge and wiped along the window still.

"Why, that Ida—Whatshername—going to be there?"

"Ida Blavatnik's a basket case, but she handles all the money in school for art supplies, so that's why I took her out a few times."

"She's very aggressive. She already put ideas in your head of leaving home."

"She only said that a man my age should try to get his own apartment."

"And who knows what else?"

**"What else is what? Will you leave me alone with this crazy talk? I'm forgetting to pack my underwear."**

**Kopfelman swung a bag off the bed and was dragged off by the momentum and the weight of it, his glasses slipping down off his nose and leaking sweat from every pore.**

**"I'll be a wreck by the time I leave if you don't calm down and stop nudgering me. Where the hell's Papa? Where's the car?"**

**"He had to go to a funeral."**

**"Are you kidding me?" Kopfelman stared at her in disbelief. "Just an hour ago, he was sitting here eating a latke sandwich and telling me what a failure I was."**

**"He didn't say failure."**

**"He called me a flop."**

**"That wasn't what he was talking about."**

**His father, at the height of rapture, never knew what he was talking about. He would sit there like a wizened, white version of Sammy Davis, Jr., and come up with lies and bullshit stories his mother would swear to, and then would both deny what was said the very next day—or sometimes, in emergencies, the very next minute.**

**"He said that he would drive me to the airport."**

**"He must've forgotten his friend was dead."**

**"I'm dying here and he's first remembering other people he knows are dead?"**

**"He'll be back in time."**

**"In time for what, my menopause?"**

**"Mr. Wiseguy, watch your language with me. Your father comes from a long line of rabbis whose words were steeped in the wisdom of scripture."**

**"I don't need a rabbi, I need a ride."**

**"You'll take a cab."**

**"They charge double fare to go to the airport."**

**"So what would you do if you lived alone and had to pay double for everything with this—Ida Blavatnik?"**

**"Will you please forget about Ida Blavatnik?"**

**"I have nothing against your getting involved with a nice Jewish girl, but marriage is also double fare!"**

**"I'll take the cab."**

**"You should only take a little consideration for me." His mother sat down and clutched her chest. *"Oy a broche."***

**"What's the matter now?"**

**"I have such a pain."**

**"What kind of pain?"**

**"What else?" she frowned. "You want me to draw a picture for you, that we sent you to college to be an artist?"**

**Kopfelman disappeared in the bathroom and used a towel to mop his face. Maybe Gregor Samsa was better off as a goddamn bug, though he knew that his mother's prohibitive love and imminent threats of acute angina were elements in a comic world he had yet to decline, let alone escape.**

**"What would you do if I changed into a cockroach?"**

**"A cockroach? Where...?"**

**"Forget about it."**

**But too late, she was there with the Raid and a golf club that he used on walks to discourage muggers.**

**"I don't see a thing."**

**"It disappeared. It heard you were coming," Kopfelman kibitzed.**

**"I clean the house on my hands and knees…"**

**"Don't kill anyone with my number 3 iron, I'm calling a cab."**

**A half hour later, the cab pulled away as Kopfelman's father swerved in the driveway, shouting and waving a fist at him. "Schmuck, you couldn't wait for me? Come back, already."**

**"Who is that guy?" the cabbie asked.**

**"He used to be a relief pitcher for the New York Mets, but then he refused to shave his beard, so they let him go."**

**"He looks like a rabbi."**

**"What else can you do when your arm goes dead."**

**"Do you want me to go back for him?"**

**"No, keep on going."**

**"Where we going?"**

**"Kennedy Airport."**

**"Double fare."**

**"I know all about it."**

**"Well, some people think I'm taking advantage and throw a fit. They're cheap as shit."**

**"Can you go any faster? I am running late."**

**"You on vacation?"**

**"I'm on Parole."**

**"I know what you mean," the cabbie laughed. "I'm married myself."**

**As the cabbie talked and went on about his wife and family, Kopfelman let his mind drift off and closed his eyes, a premonitory breeze from the window, running and gunning his hair about, and reaffirming his sudden liberation and freedom…the long-awaited sultry nights of thronging street fairs and fireworks, exotic women, chance encounters, the erotic thrum of the Mardi Gras…**

**"No, I don't believe in going back."**

**"Going back where?"**

**"To anywhere," Kopfelman answered the cabbie, though really more in answer to himself than anything else for the gathering dusk had spread through every haunt of him like angel dust and made him aware of immensities inside himself that had yet to be filled, and which nothing so far had defined in him.**

**"Ulysses S. Grant once wrote in his memoirs," Kopfelman noticed the cabdriver staring suspiciously in the rearview mirror, "that he didn't believe in turning back no matter how badly lost he got. That for him the Past Tense didn't exist, and that rather than try to retrace his steps and have to start all over again, he would always forge on blindly ahead and take his chances."**

**"Who the hell is Ulysses S. Grant?"**

**"You never heard of the name before?"**

**"Is he somebody I should know about?"**

**Kopfelman smiled and thought of his father pitching for the New York Mets.**

**"He used to be big in basketball."**

**The cabbie swerved to avoid a bus.**

**"I gotcha," he said. "A shvartza, yeah. Those people pick out fucking names like nobody's business."**

∞○∞

## 3

In Abruzzi, there was deep confusion. Domestic strife. The Strangler's wife was beside herself.

"I don't want you dying in no country with Spics! You wanna drop dead? You do it at home with your own family here and not in some godforsaken place where we don't even know if they'll send back your body."

"Shut up, Theresa, you talk too much."

"Yeah, tell me to shut up somemore," she grew defiant, "and what am I gonna tell your children, that we don't even know where your father is to put flowers on his grave?"

"Stop burying me."

"You'll never come back, and you know that better than anyone else, so who are you fooling?"

"*Sta'tente*—listen carefully to me. There's half a million dollars involved if I do it right. In *lira*, do you know what that means? They'd have to fill up the back of a coal truck to bring it to you!" This silenced her as he lumbered to the refrigerator and

**tore off the top of a can of beer. "I still got my strength to do the job, but in six more months I'll be shitting all over the floor and blankets, so listen to me and don't say another fucking word until I finish, capito?"**

**"Si..."**

**A crucifix on the wall of the kitchen loomed overhead like a helicopter.**

**"Whatever money I get from the job goes straight to you from Don Vincenzo."**

**"But what if you don't come back from the job?"**

**"Shut up, I said!"**

**He explained to her the "ins" and "outs" and vicissitudes of the deal he had made.**

**"If I don't come back and can't do the job, you get half the money no matter what! If I do the job, under any conditions, you're gonna end up with all of it."**

**"But you're not gonna be here."**

**"So what?" he barked. "I'm not gonna be here anyway."**

**He slammed his fist at the kitchen wall and blew apart a hole in it the size of his armpit.**

**"Nunzio, please, don't lose your temper."**

**"I think I'm getting one of my fits, quick, tie me up."**

**The ropes came out. She bound him with the help of her sons who sat on him and shoved a piece of wood in his mouth as he thrashed and foamed and blacked out into stiffening waves of frenzied homicidal convulsions.**

**Nothing was said until Mrs. Zangara had given the nod which meant they could all go back to living.**

**"Whatta you watching on television?"**

**"Gilligan's Island."**

**"All right," she said, "go back inside. It's over now."**

**The moment that the trembling ceased, she positioned herself with a pair of pliers and carefully removed all the slivers of wood that had lodged in his teeth, as well as those he had chewed into splinters.**

**"Nunzio, are you all right, dear?"**

**"Get the ropes off me."**

**"Are you hungry?"**

**"Yeah, but don't make me nothing too hard to eat, my teeth feel loose..."**

**She undid the ropes and busied herself at the stove for him, God bless his soul! Whenever he had these crazy attacks, or killed someone, his appetite always seemed to improve.**

**"And when are you gonna leave on this trip?"**

**"I leave tomorrow," he stuffed his mouth with arugula salad. "Pass me the bread."**

**She sat down beside him to watch him eat and started to cry.**

**"Stop acting like a *scooch'a'menza*," Nunzio forked the loaf of bread. "We had twenty-seven good years together."**

**"But half of them you spent in jail."**

**"Don't talk so loud."**

**"The kids can't hear."**

**"I don't want nobody knowing my business."**

**"After all these years, you don't think your sons are suspicious of you that you don't have a regular working job?"**

**"I'm a traveling salesman."**

**"Yeah," she said, "and everyone knows that you don't sell nothing. Whatta you think these kids are dumb? We gave them plenty of education in all the best schools."**

**"And all they do is watch television and sit on my chest when I have attacks."**

**"As long as they don't get in trouble, Nunzio, that means that we did our job. That's the most important thing of all, so whatta you complaining about?"**

**"All right, shut up, I don't wanna start no arguments here," he conciliated. "There's something I wanna tell you about while I still have time." He rose to his feet and wiped his mouth with a deadly look of abiding affection and deep concern. "In all the years that we been together…I never been unfaithful to you with another woman, and that's the truth. Just remember that."**

**"I know," she said. "A woman could always know these things without being told."**

**"I don't wanna hear no bullshit talk!" he grew irritated. "Why do you always contradict me?"**

**"Who's contradicting?"**

**"I'm trying to tell you in all these years, I always had respect for you. *I always loved you…*" he screamed at her. "Don't you understand a fucking thing I say to you?"**

**"Que bedu!" she cried, and fell to the floor and kissed his feet.**

**"All right...all right...Put the pasta on and don't make a goddamn fool of yourself. I gotta go."**

**"But Nunzio, you don't have to go. The money don't mean nothing to me."**

**"You say that now, but five years from now you'll be cursing yourself and cursing me...and this time I'm gonna drown you in money. I'll make you rich."**

**She sobbed and quickly covered her face so he wouldn't see her, and rearranged all the candles in her Novena stand.**

**"Are you sure Don Vincenzo will send me the money once you're...well, you know what I mean."**

**"When I'm dead, you mean. Just say what you mean!"**

**"I don't wanna say it."**

**"Then whatta you saying?" his neck veins popped.**

**He had never ever considered before that Don Vincenzo would not make good his word to him. The thought had never crossed his mind. "Don Vincenzo is a simple man who goes by his rules. He thinks of himself as *Un Uomo Respitato*, and not only does he believe in God, he believes that there is life after death, that stupid fuck—and if there is—and he doesn't pay up what's coming to you, I'll come back from hell and tear his fucking *cugliones* out!"**

**"*Que dio mio*, God forbid! Don't talk that way."**

**"Then why do you put these ideas in my head when you know how fucking crazy it gets me, you sonofabitch."**

**"I'll make you some pasta."**

**"Fongoo'la pasta!"**

**"Nunzio, please, what's the matter with you?"**

**"Come over here..."**

**She well understood the command involved and gave up a sigh of the living dead and prayed to God and smacked her head, but with Nunzio there was no reprieve and no way out the moment he had that look on his face. The very same look that had chilled her down to her ankle bones the first time she saw it—and recognized only too well now in the murderous gleam of bloodshot eyes that twisted along the swollen ridge and veins of his forehead, splitting his face into No Man's Land, into darkened realms she had had to withstand in mute surrender, martyred silence...meekly... sadly...stooping her way down the narrow stairs to the food storage room, where he took her standing against the wall as he did on the night of his very first kill.**

ooo

**On the following night, in the most expensive, lavish hotel in Rio de Janeiro, he anxiously rose from a dream-laden sleep of unrelieved nightmares—and feeling the urge to kill someone and wreck every piece of ugly fucking homosexual furniture in the room, decided to go for a midnight swim and work out his anger in order to be in total control for the meeting that day with Don Vincenzo's daughter and son, though something about this entire**

**setup was bothering him. He couldn't quite put it together in his mind, but the idea of having to lie and scheme and throw himself on the mercy of others to get at Big Al Gavona was not only like a kick in the balls but an insult to his whole reputation and way of life, and beyond that was the humiliation of going there like a little queer with a thumb up his ass and offering to betray the Don! You had to suck cock to play that part. You had to be someone with tits and cunt and no fucking conscience.**

**Nunzio felt a pain in his chest. A deep down rattling noisy sensation that seemed to take all his breath away and cut into his arms and legs. He hoped it wasn't another one of his fits coming on, especially now when he needed every ounce of strength to do the job and do it right, and now he was getting these warning signs that were all mixed up and new to him, and why the fuck were his teeth getting big?**

**He raced outside to get some air before something really exploded in him and bolted down the steep descent of uneven steps that led to the deck of the promenade, which was numbingly stretched out in all directions and fairly deserted except for occasional strolling couples who glanced up in alarm at him as he paused in flight, a bath towel clutched in his right hand fist and gasping…almost completely dazed and fighting for every breath of air, his right eye starting to close on him when he spotted someone off in the distance who looked like he was out of his mind: a boardwalk figure ridiculously dressed in evening clothes—and swinging a golf club!**

**What the hell kind of place was this?**

**What kind of fucking deranged kind of people came to these resorts?**

**Anything crazy could happen here with all these nutjobs floating around.**

**He even drew out a laugh from this as he headed toward the boardwalk stairs leading down to the beach and remembered the time he had whacked someone out in the parking lot in Las Vegas somewhere, and came close to getting killed himself when some woman driver backed out her car unexpectedly and almost made the hit on *him.* Which he thought about with the same amusement and easing of pain he had always felt when dealing with the unexpected, digging his feet in the cooling sand by the water's edge and neatly wrapping his clothes in the towel along with his room key and personal possessions. Still on edge, but lulled by the sound of ocean breakers cutting across the darkness to him and urging him to relax for a moment...unbend a little...lower his guard...like a woman slowly disrobing herself and leading him on while somebody stuck a knife in his back, those no-good, whore, bastard bitches...**

***Fighiu di Butana*!**

**He gripped his chest and felt the thrust of evil again knifing into him as he whirled about instinctively toward the promenade and the rapid sound of clicking heels at the rear of the figure in evening clothes—who even before he had time to react or call for help was instantly mugged and hurled out over the parapet of the**

**boardwalk railing, tumbling onto the sand below in a headlong dive that actually made the Strangler gasp in astonishment.**

**The men who had done it were shouting to each other and wantonly waving a wallet around as though they hadn't a fear in the world of being caught, those no-good, lowlife scombadella. What a disgrace! What an insult to his own profession. What the hell kind of place was this? It was true that he had killed and even maimed for a living, but never in an elegant resort with family and friends and vacationing couples, who maybe saved their entire lives to go on a trip and enjoy themselves.**

***Que Porco de Miseria!***

**There was no longer any sense of structure. Nobody played by the rules anymore. The young people did whatever they wanted and nobody gave a shit anymore for anything of enduring values—Parents, Country, the Organization...the whole fucking world was falling apart, and Nunzio was roaring mad. He had even considered chasing the muggers and breaking their backs, but he couldn't risk the exposure involved in case he might be recognized by someone who knew him and word got back, so reluctantly he resigned himself and made his peace, made the sign of the cross (which he only did at funerals or right after having killed somebody) and plunged into the greater darkness lying ahead. The bruise of the ocean striking at him in wave after wave like the hand of God pouring over him, only much too late for the upward climb into cleansing absolution and grace, for God didn't seem to give a shit either...and all he could think of was "What a**

**joke" as the sickening blow he had least expected came tearing out of his lungs and chest…and blew him back into nothingness.**

∞∞

# 4

**At eight in the morning, the beachfront of the *Praia da Gavea* in Rio de Janeiro was still deserted, the high glitz and the alabaster airdrome of luxury hotels staring vacantly at an ocean view of thundering breakers, not as in all the tourist posters, but overcast with threatening clouds and darkened skies; a few stray tourists drifting along the horseshoe crescent of gleaming white sand, and gathering slowly, drawn as though magnetically to the gruesome sight of a huge bloated body in bathing trunks being zippered into a canvas bag while baffled police and an ambulance corps of rescue squad attendants shouted back and forth in torrents of a native dialect that seemed always to verge on the edge of a violence greater than that which had claimed the life of the burly bather whose body had been washed up onshore so mysteriously.**

**Eventually, they had blundered upon the only link they could make to the body, a bath towel wrapped with personal effects: a ribbed hose undertop, bedroom slippers, dark wool pants, a worn**

**leather wallet with lottery tickets and incidental cash, and wedged in between the folds of the wallet, a passport with a picture of the deceased in it that looked like a mug shot of someone out of an Abnormal Psych book.**

**On the body itself, there were numerous scars and one clear mark of identification adorning its rear, in the region of the left posterior gluteus maximus, a tattoo in the shape of a fist with criss-cross daggers and dangling snakes that read: A Fongoo.**

**At a further remove from all this confusion, Kopfelman, who was sprawled out on a stretch of sand underneath the boardwalk and hidden from view, had painfully stirred into consciousness, the blare of horns and screeching wheels of departing vehicles waking him to a fine piss drizzle and no recollection of where he was or what he was doing with a lump on his head and all of his pockets turned inside out. He couldn't even remember his name...**

**Was it possible that he had no name?**

**He stumbled up and groped forward blindly, searching the sand for something that might belong to him—some little trace, no matter how small or inconsequential—and thus redeem who he was to himself.**

**When he reached the spot where the dead man had been whisked away, he stubbed his toe on a sharp metal object and picked up what appeared to be, upon closer inspection, a room key with the imprint of a hotel name and room number on it.**

**How had he dropped it so far away?**

**He continued searching but nothing else materialized, so he trudged to the boardwalk, still slightly dazed and wondering where on earth he was, and eventually reached the promenade where street hawkers flung their wares at him and cabdrivers soon encircled him who were willing to take him anywhere, especially if he wanted a woman—or maybe two women—or maybe he liked to watch animals?**

**"Does anyone speak English here?"**

**"Si, senor."**

**"What is this place? What country is this?"**

**The cabdrivers seemed amused by this and a half hour later one of them deposited him at the hotel on the room key tag, two hundred feet from where they had originally started.**

**"This place looks familiar."**

**"Everything looks familiar here."**

**"I think I've been mugged."**

**"You don't like the way I take you here? You call the police. I know all the police."**

**"That's not what I'm saying. I don't have my wallet. I have to go up to my room for money."**

**"I come with you."**

**They marched through the lobby and made their way to the room in question—201—and as Kopfelman turned the key in the latch and heard it click open, he felt simultaneously panic stricken and deeply relieved.**

**"You wait here, yes?"**

**The driver nodded and planted his feet in the frame of the doorway as Kopfelman tentatively searched through some drawers that had underwear, socks, some gaudy colored handpainted ties...then reached in the closet and went through the pockets of a huge beige suit that was hanging there and found some bills. Five thousand pesetas. How much that was in American money he had no idea, but he knew he was thinking in dollars and cents and that something about the thought of money was bothering him.**

**"How much do I owe you?"**

**"A thousand pesetas."**

**"That's a pretty expensive cab ride."**

**"Yeah, well whatta you think, we're cheap in this country?"**

**Kopfelman paid and shut the door of what had to be a luxury suite with a terrace overlooking the ocean. Very impressive. A man would have to do very well to afford this place. He wondered what line of work he was in and continued searching the drawers and closets, and picked his way through some half-opened luggage, an overnight flight bag, and something sealed in a plastic wrap that looked like a disemboweled cock but which turned out to be a roll of Soprasada salami.**

**He blinked his eyes and tried to gather his wits about him.**

**"There must be a passport somewhere around here."**

**But maybe that's what they took when they mugged him, along with his wallet and all his money—and what the hell was**

**wrong with him? Every move he made or step he took, he kept bumping into the furniture.**

**It was then that he spotted the letter from Abruzzi, Italy, moldering at the bottom of the overnight bag, and addressed to someone named Nunzio—or was that the name of another town?**

> **"...and we figured because of your condition out there, you would take the risk and get back to us either way about it because nobody else will do it for us, and you always done very good for us in the past, so please keep in touch since you ain't got no phone and that is the reason I'm writing this letter. My father sends his regards to you.**
>
> **Carmine M."**

**Who on earth was Carmine M. and what was he doing with this letter in his room?**

**He read it again and started to get a splitting headache. Maybe if he took a shower and went to sleep, he would wake up knowing all the right answers, or at least not feel like passing out. He fought off the feeling, removed himself from the oversized shell of his evening clothes (which clumped to the floor as though two other men were undressing beside him), and just as he was about to strip down to his underwear, caught sight of himself in the mirrored alcove—and jumped in fright.**

**Who the hell was that?**

**Kopfelman peeked and squinted back at the haggard-looking, nondescript features and tentative slope of the chin and mouth, as though viewing the corpse of an accident victim and daring the**

image to strike at something familiar in him, but he couldn't relate to any of this, and liked even less the stick-thin arms flexing back at him from the mirrored wall like two pathetic, love-starved and enfeebled orphans.

How the hell had this happened to him?

Was he sick or something?

Kopfelman gripped the back of his neck and rolled up his eyes in a ritual form of hysteria that he knew had some essential link to who he was, and what he was, but no longer felt the need to recall. Enough was enough! He was so depressed he could hardly remove his underwear—and especially not in front of the mirror.

After such knowledge, what forgiveness?

"Maybe it's better I don't remember," he sighed to himself, for even as he entered the shower and tried to drown out all his thoughts in torrents of water, he could not ignore the obvious fact that "remembering" was the downfall of almost everyone who had ever gotten screwed in life, and without any memory of past or future to hold him back or worry about, he was innocent. The slate was clean. It was almost like being reborn again in an infinite and euphoric state of present potential, free of any doubt or fear or recrimination, for now he could start all over again whatever it was he had never begun—and to hell with all the rest of it.

So what if he didn't like his looks and didn't know what he was doing here with a lump on his head and taking a shower in Rio de Janeiro? Who cared anymore? What else could possible

**happen to him that would offset, even remotely for him, this shining moment of sudden illumination and insight?**

**Kopfelman sang and beat his chest and was onto something so profound, his cock flew up and frightened him as the telephone rang.**

**Was it room service or a personal call?**

**He jumped from the shower, dripping wet, and got tangled up in the telephone cord while trying to get at a bathroom towel to wipe himself off.**

**"Yes?" he answered, waiting for the unknown to declare itself at the other end. "Who is this, please?"**

**"Nunzio?"**

**Kopfelman scanned the room. Did the man whose name appeared on the letter live here too?**

**"Yes...who is this?" he strung out noncommittally.**

**"It's Josephine, Don Vincenzo's daughter. I'm here with my brother Carmine," she said. "Are you decent?"**

**"Well, I just took a shower..."**

**"That's okay," she said. "I'm calling you from another room in the same hotel. We'll give you some time to make a change."**

**He ran in circles, looking through all the unpacked clothes in the half-opened luggage and wondering who these people were who were looking for this Nunzio fellow: Josephine, Carmine, Don Vincenzo...what names they had!...and then he remembered the letter with this Carmine's name and read it again, and opened**

**the closet and tried on a pair of green checkered pants that fit him like a Ringling Brothers circus tent.**

**Was it possible he had lost this much weight since coming out here?**

**The doorbell rang and Kopfelman froze as he opened the door and gazed at the face of a towering beauty who dwarfed him by comparison. She nodded tersely, flicked her eyes judgmentally, and swept by him as though he didn't exist at all. As though she were part of some ancient order of *Women Beyond the Reach of Men*, remote and unattainable. Behind her was a man with scars and pushed-in nose who was almost as tall as the frame of the doorway.**

**"You're not looking well," she appraised him coldly.**

**Kopfelman watched her every move in astonishment. She was dressed in white and the pleated folds of her undulant body gave rise to such intensely erotic radiation that the heat of it had inflamed his nose and clogged up all his sinuses.**

**"I sort of had an accident," he apologized dumbly.**

**"How?" she asked. "What happened to you?"**

**He was too embarrassed to say he'd been mugged.**

**"I think I must have blacked out or something and hit my head." She looked like the type who would hound you to death and bit off your head if you even so much as blinked at her, which is just the sort of woman he loved and had worshiped blindly all his life in his own inveterate horniness. "Just an hour ago, I**

**couldn't even remember my name or what I was even doing here."**

**She could not disguise the contempt she felt for this lowlife vermin, feared throughout the underworld. She knew all about his episodic bouts of destruction. Many an unsuspecting victim—including friends and relatives—had paid the price during one of Nunzio's infamous "blackouts."**

**"I must admit, you look nothing like I thought you would."**

**"Yeah, we pictured you as a much bigger man," Carmine gestured solemnly. He measured with an arm raised high above his head exactly what he was talking about. "My father said you was stronger than any ten men he knew."**

**"Which is why you were the one man who was chosen for the job," Josephine added. "That, of course, and unfortunately—the other thing. My father sends his deepest regret."**

**Regret for what? He had no idea what was going on.**

**"What other thing? I don't know what you're talking about."**

**There was deadly silence. Josephine tried to size things up without appearing ridiculous. She had heard about the Strangler's moods and interludes of incoherence, but this was beginning to wear on her. Could it possibly be he was playing a game and testing them?**

**"Are you serious?"**

**"Yes, I told you before, I hit my head and I don't remember anything about anything."**

She could see the bruise and discoloration. "Mind if I have a look at it?"

"Be careful," he winced. "Don't press too hard, it really hurts."

"Believe me, I'll be careful," she smiled, though each new disclosure was so disarming, so far removed from what she had heard and expected of him, that only by force of will alone was she able to restrain herself from laughing in his goomba face and letting him know what she thought of him, which is not what she was sent here to do, and most certainly not what her father would have expected of her, for Don Vincenzo had always issued a solemn injunction regarding the matter of psychopaths: The most dangerous men were the ones who looked like the kitchen help. The tough guys and all the gorilla types he used for enforcement and cleanup jobs (including Carmine) had at one time or other fainted away at the thought of having to kill someone, so she couldn't afford to indulge herself or ever make the dread mistake of miscalculating this wimp-like appearance and attitude as anything less than a possible front for disarming people.

"Yes," she said, "I must admit that's quite a blow. I think we have serious problems here."

Her brother gave a look of alarm.

"Do you think that anyone's wise to this? Could it be that maybe the word's leaked out?"

"Stop panicking!" she dismissed abruptly. "Nobody knows what Nunzio looks like, only the people he's put away."

**"Then what the hell's going on over here?"**

**"You think I know?"**

**Exhausted, Kopfelman flopped in a chair, his brief fling at being reborn again expiring into the dampening folds of his underwear, along with all its infinite and euphoric potential.**

**"I'm also getting pretty bad headaches."**

**"How did it happen?" Carmine asked. "It looks worse to me than a blackout spell. I mean, where did you get that crack on your head?"**

**Kopfelman nodded sheepishly.**

**"I think I was mugged."**

**"They mugged you?"**

**"Well, I don't exactly remember," he said, "but I must have been walking along the beach, maybe late at night, and the next thing I knew, I woke up with a lump on my head and all my pockets inside out."**

**"It's incredible, really!" Josephine rose and paced the room. It had all gone wrong and somehow, she knew, she would end up getting blamed for this. "The Abruzzi Strangler mugged on the beach! That's something to write home about..." She angrily lit up a cigarette and exhaled into Kopfelman's face. "You don't remember anything at all? The plans we made? What we're doing out here?"**

**"I only remember what I told you," he said. He was starting to shiver and shake inside and suddenly realized his chest was bare and dripping wet. "Would you please excuse me?"**

**Kopfelman crossed to the chrome-paneled dresser and put on a shirt that reached to his knees. "I think I must have...amnesia...or something..."**

**"Amnesia shit!" Carmine pulled out a gun from his belt that looked much too real. "We paid you a quarter million bucks to do this job, and you better not pull no crap on us."**

**"Carmine, put that thing away and just relax."**

**"I don't like what's going on over here."**

**"Well, neither do I, but you're not helping matters by acting like an imbecile."**

**The situation had suddenly grown impossible, and the "X" factor that her father had always talked about, the unknown and the variables involved, were in no way reaping rewards in her mind as she struggled to contain herself and reassess the game plan that no longer existed.**

**Kopfelman felt a deepening pain inside his groin.**

**"I don't think I've ever killed anyone."**

**"Of course you have."**

**"You see what the fuck I'm talking about?" Carmine exploded.**

**"Shut up," she said, "and let me talk."**

**She carefully laid out the groundwork again to Kopfelman.**

**"I'm going to give you some background stuff on why you're here, and maybe something will ring a bell."**

**"I'll ring the fucking bell for him," Carmine challenged.**

**"My father," Josephine warned him off, "is in terrible danger. His life has been threatened. Two years ago, he decided to relinquish any sort of business he had in drug-related holdings and give it over to the Orientals."**

**"The fucking Chinks!" Carmine quickly corrected.**

**"Which immediately had a ripple effect," she warned again, "since the New York families dealt mostly with South America for all their supplies, and now that the...Chinks had taken over, they naturally went to their own suppliers for a lot less money on the wholesale end, and a staggering loss of billions of dollars in distribution for Big Al Gavona."**

**She then explained who Big Al was and lit up another cigarette by biting down on the filter part with all the allure of something erotic. "So the fat man put out a contract on my father that luckily failed, but which proved to be very costly in lives and threatened to escalate even further if other attempts were bound to be made, so a council was called and Big Al's tactics were overruled in favor of getting rid of him."**

**"That fucking strunz," Carmine acknowledged. "He should'a been put away long ago, but no one around would take the job of whacking him out 'cause he lives on an island so heavily guarded that anyone who would be lucky enough to get through to him and do the job, would never live to tell about it."**

**"In other words, we were looking for the impossible. A suicide mission with no way out..." She paused to let the full weight of the implication settle on him and searched about for**

**something to drink, but then she remembered the Strangler neither drank nor smoked—and judging by his current condition, had apparently given up fucking too. "We contacted you because word was out you were so far gone and terminally ill, you had nothing to lose by taking the job, so my father arranged to pay all the money, your end of it, to your wife and children and..."**

**"Wait a minute," Kopfelman moaned. "A wife and children I don't remember, but whoever said I was terminally ill?"**

**"I only know what my father told me."**

**"What did he tell you?"**

**"He said you had cancer...and six months to live."**

**"You mean I'm actually dying?" he choked.**

**She chose to ignore the obvious answer.**

**"I'm sorry," she said, "but I didn't mean to upset you this way."**

**"Upset me?" Kopfelman sputtered and spit all over Carmine across the way. "Why should losing my life be upsetting? An hour ago, I only had a bump on my head, and now I have only six months to live! I mean, why not break out a bottle or something and drink to my health?"**

**"You got any Scotch," Carmine wiped himself off, "or you gonna go on spraying me here?"**

**"Will you shut up already?" Josephine warned. "The man is on the verge of a breakdown. He doesn't remember anything."**

**"How could anybody forget that he's dying? You gotta be outta your fucking mind."**

***"Sta muta."***

**"Yeah. *Ugatz'in gool*!"**

**And while both of them were attacking each other, Kopfelman burrowed deeper and deeper inside himself, until he assumed a fetal position all his own, rocking back and forth as though he were sitting *Shiva* for himself.**

**No wonder he looked so all fucked up and undernourished and none of his clothing would fit on him. It was all so insane, he could hardly breathe or catch his breath...a wife and children...killing people...six months to live...**

**He leaned back with his eyes rolled up inside his head as though he had just been executed. How did this ever happen to him? He remembered something deep in his past about stealing something, maybe it was a piece of candy...in Julie's drugstore...a peanut brittle he shoved in his coat when he should have been in school that day...or was it *Shul*?—and what did it mean to be sitting *Shiva*?**

**Josephine led her brother onto the terrace outside.**

**"Will you listen to me for just a minute? Stop arguing. I need your help."**

**"Just remember who you're talking to," he cautioned her. "I'm the oldest here, and I don't like it when you start giving me orders and boss me around."**

**"All right, I'm sorry."**

**"You always gotta have your own way."**

**She let him rant and rave at her until he had finally run out of steam.**

**"What do you think of the mess we have? You think he can do the job for us?"**

**"The fucking guy looks like Woody Allen."**

**"That's not what I mean."**

**"He looks like he's ready for the fucking grave."**

**"I'm going to go ahead with this."**

**"You're outta your mind."**

**"The only thing we have to lose is already lost." She motioned over at Kopfelman, then waved to him. "We'll be just a second."**

**"I think we oughta call Poppa about this."**

**"I know what I'm doing."**

**"You're throwing his fucking money away."**

**"It's his life that we ought to be worried about."**

**"You always gotta fucking win."**

**"Have I ever been wrong?" she threw up at him.**

**"Okay," he said. "We'll give it a shot.**

**They both returned to Kopfelman.**

**"Well," she said, "are you feeling any better now?"**

**"I feel as though my head's coming off."**

**"Aside from that, are there any other questions you have, any lingering doubts?"**

**"Well, whoever mugged me must have taken more than my wallet. I have no identification on me."**

**"Your identification is in your hands, that's all you have to worry about."**

**"You better tell him the plan again so there ain't no unexpected slipups," Carmine ordered.**

**Josephine reached inside her purse for an envelope and placed it on the cocktail table near Kopfelman's chair.**

**"That should hold you awhile. The hotel room is all taken care of, and everything else that was promised to you."**

**"And what am I supposed to do?"**

**"You're *defecting*!" Carmine savored the word (he had learned it in a James Bond movie). "You're going over to the other side as a double agent."**

**Kopfelman didn't get the connection.**

**"Am I still supposed to strangle this guy as a double agent?"**

**"No, you go there and tickle his ass with a feather!" Carmine bellowed. "Whatta you kidding? You get your fucking hands on his neck and choke him to death."**

**Josephine drew a seat for herself across the way and tried to tone things down a bit.**

**"Big Al will think you're selling out. You'll contact him and tell him what you were hired to do, but that once you thought it over to yourself and realized the hit was impossible, you decided on double indemnity; that is, going over to the other side for equal pay in exchange for information."**

**"In other words, I should make them think I'm on their side before getting killed?'**

**"So the Strangler does have a sense of humor," Josephine cracked.**

**"Is that what they call me?"**

**"Everyone knows your reputation."**

**"What makes you think they'll believe that story?"**

**"This!" she said, and brandished what looked like a dog-eared copy of the Gutenberg Bible. "Big Al would give his right arm for this. It's your passport into that fortress of his."**

**Kopfelman leafed through page after page of handwritten entries.**

**"All I see are recipes here for Italian food."**

**"But Italian food like nobody's ever eaten before," Carmine leered, "and we even got something better than that."**

**His sister removed from the depths of her bag an evil-looking, cast-iron frying pan, aged with layers and layers of grease.**

**"These are our strategic weapons," Josephine explained to him, "because Big Al Gavona's passion is food, and when Al and my father first started out by working their way up through the Organization, doing jobs together, rooming together, and cooking for the mob, the one thing that really bugged him the most was that, try as he might, he could never cook as well as my father, Don Vincenzo, who always had that something special, that extra touch that Big Al was missing in his own preparation of the meals he made, and even when he made it to the top as the kingpin of drugs in South America, it really tore him up inside that my father's food was always considered the best in the business.**

**Lucky Luciano traveled two thousand miles for my father's Osso Buco de Vincenzo!"**

**"And even when he tried to have my father killed," Carmine interjected angrily, "getting hold of my father's cookbook was also a part of the contract he put out on him, which, believe me, is considered patza in our line of work, even by people who are very sick."**

**Josephine played out the rest of it.**

**"Let's just say that the fat man has the hots for it, and to show good faith in going over to the other side, you're going to offer up all these goodies as compensation."**

**Kopfelman reached for the frying pan.**

**"It's heavy."**

**"Yeah? Well, the pan may be more important than the book!" Carmine admonished. "You know how long it's been in the family? You know how many years of flavor is blended in there from cooking and shit?"**

**"My father broke down and almost cried when he let it go."**

**"That's how bad he wants to get this guy."**

**"It's your calling card."**

**"And once that asshole buys into that and takes you in…"**

**Josephine finished the thought for him by playfully reaching for Kopfelman's throat.**

**"You'll have him right in those hands of yours!"**

**But Kopfelman (who was simultaneously undergoing the numbing effect of Josephine's sensuous stranglehold, while**

fighting off a full-scale erection that threatened to launch the entire room) had not the slightest inclination toward murder or mayhem or making lasagna, and if it was true he had only such a short time to live and was doomed to die so ingloriously, he would gladly have had her dance on his chest with stiletto heels and stomp him to death, while waiting for the end to come.

"It's sitting there right in your fucking lap," Carmine lauded. "All you gotta do is squeeze when the right time comes. There's just no way you can miss with this!"

"You make it sound easy."

"It won't be easy," Josephine shoved her brother aside. "Carmine gets carried away sometimes and exaggerates, but lots of thought has gone into this, and who could have known you'd black out that way or have this loss of memory?" She probed again the lump on his head with needle-sharp lacquered fingernails that seemed to encompass half his brain and all his nerves. "All we're doing is trying to help reorient you and build up your confidence, make things as simple as possible for you."

Kopfelman heard not a word of this. He was overwhelmed by an aching sensation so bittersweet and tinged with longing, it surged through every part of him, every nook and cranny of places he'd never lived before, and which Josephine now brought home to him so hypnotically in lethal waves of Shalomar that threatened to unhinge his soul with each accidental brush of her body.

"Tell me," he said, "do you have any children?"

**Josephine narrowed an eye at him and stiffened immediately.**

**"What do you mean? What difference does it make?"**

**"Hey, keep your fucking mind on the job!" Carmine rose up protectively and hitched his pants. "You watch out how you talk to my sister."**

**"All I said was…"**

**"Fuck what you said!"**

**"I was just being friendly."**

**"Fuck your friendship," Carmine challenged. "I don't wanna hear no bullshit from you. I know all about you Abruzzese. Just watch your mouth."**

**"Why, what are you going to do about it?" Kopfelman almost turned to see who was talking. "You going to kill a dying man and take on Mr. Fatman yourself?"**

**"You asshole!" Carmine lunged at him. "You really think you're so fucking funny."**

**Josephine thrust her body between them and held onto her brother's arm.**

**"Nunzio's right, he didn't mean anything disrespectful."**

**"Who's Nunzio?" Kopfelman smiled at her, and Carmine almost bit off her head in trying to reach out and grab at him.**

**"That's you—you prick!"**

**"Carmine, stop it, what're you doing?" Josephine tried to hold him back.**

**"He can't even remember his fucking name—he's an invalid. We oughta call this whole thing off."**

**"Will you please calm down?" She dragged off into a corner with him. "What's wrong with you?"**

**"The man is a nut job. He don't make sense. I'm calling Papa."**

**"And what do you think he's going to say? Get somebody else to do the job that only a nut job would even consider?"**

**Reluctantly, Carmine got the drift and resigned himself.**

**"In other words, we're stuck with this fucking gagoocha here."**

**"He's not as dumb as you think he is. It's just that maybe he's still in shock."**

**"And when the hell is he gonna wake up and snap out of it?"**

**"Do you have to curse like an animal?"**

**"Okay, okay...but it's not gonna work, you mark my words. There's something very wrong about this. In fact, it stinks, and I'm telling you, Josie, I don't like having to tell a guy his own fucking business when it's costing us a fortune here."**

**"Just leave it to me. I know what I'm doing."**

**Carmine shook his head in disgust and lowered a look at Kopfelman that was meant to kill.**

**"You're lucky that my sister's here."**

**"We'll be back later." Josephine led her brother to the door and eased into a Don Vincenzo's daughter smile. "Just remember that we're in this together, we're all here together to do a job, so get some rest."**

**Kopfelman nodded glumly at her and groped about for an antidote.**

**"Is it possible I can remember who I am by going to sleep?"**

**And Carmine answered loud and clear.**

**"If you don't forget to wake up, you fucking stunado, you!"**

ꝏꝏ

# 5

**At the garish American Embassy building, two elderly ladies from the United Federation of Teachers Art Convention, Mrs. Rita Covington and Yetta Epstein, had filed a report of the disappearance of one male Caucasian, Marvin Kopfelman.**

**"Are you sure he's white?" the official from the consulate asked condescendingly. "*Caucasian* doesn't mean anything today."**

**The two women turned to stare at each other bewilderedly. Mrs. Covington looked like Somerset Maugham, and Yetta had intimations about her, flirts of resemblance to Bella Abzug.**

**"Mr. Kopfelman is most definitely white," Mrs. Covington answered indignantly. "I don't understand what you're talking about."**

**"There are blacks who say they're Caucasian also."**

**"How can that be?"**

**"Just ask them about it. I'm not here to argue race with them," the official smirked. It looked like someone had locked**

**him up in a closet all his life and let him out in time for work. "Now when was the first time you noticed that this Kopfelman fellow was officially missing?"**

**"A day ago, at a formal dinner our convention held at the Rio Sheraton."**

**"A marvelous choice."**

**"Well, the price was right."**

**"Mr. Kopfelman was in attendance there?"**

**"He was there in body but not in mind. There was something eating away at him. He said he wanted a breath of air, and that's the last that we saw of him."**

**"What time was that?"**

**"Oh, sometime after midnight, I guess."**

**"We're talking about a beachfront hotel," the official sorted out for them, "where occasional guests, at one time or the other, have tried to go for a midnight swim—and never returned."**

**"Oh, no, he was wearing a full dress tuxedo."**

**"That has never been a restraining force," the official blinked. "How long has Mr. Kopfelman been gone?"**

**"Since yesterday," Mrs. Epstein answered. "We checked his room and thought it might be a good idea to bring you his passport."**

**"Are either of you officially in charge?"**

**"No, Ida Blavatnik's officially in charge, but she's also involved in arranging tours and a Mardi-Gras feast and asked us to represent her here."**

"I see," he said. "Is it possible that he might have met a woman or something?"

"Not Marvin, no, he isn't the type."

The official examined the passport photo.

"I see your point," he temporized. "What about problems? You mentioned an emotional upset."

Mrs. Covington dabbed at both her eyes with a ready-wipe.

"We don't want to sound like meddlers, you know, but he struck me as being weak and dependent, the sort of person incapable of even the smallest decisions—and haunted by fear of violence."

Mrs. Epstein nodded firmly to that.

"I remember on the trip over here, we had to assure him the plane wouldn't crash, or that none of us would be taken hostage."

"He worried a lot," Mrs. Covington added. "He worried about the state of the world, and he worried about his mother's health continually. A wonderful son. I believe he lived at home with his parents."

"At forty-two?"

"My son is forty-eight years old and lives at home," Mrs. Epstein responded angrily.

"Does he have any sort of drinking problem? Drug abuse?"

"Oh, heavens no! He's a health food addict, never drinks, he doesn't smoke, and..." Mrs. Covington lowered her voice and looked about for racial types "...the smell of any Italian cooking makes him nauseous for days on end."

**"He also had trouble breathing at times whenever anyone mentioned death," Mrs. Epstein concluded.**

**"I see…" the official noted down. "All this is very helpful, of course, but what can you tell me about this man that might be viewed suspiciously?**

**Mrs. Covington raised a dubious brow, and both women turned away to each other, as though to imply there were some things better left unsaid that they both were dying to talk about.**

**"We don't know if he believes in God," Mrs. Covington frowned, "but we do know he believes in abortion!"**

**"Abortion?"**

**"Yes."**

**The official eyed them curiously.**

**"Well, unless he's pregnant, that doesn't seem to help us much. Is there anything else?"**

**"We're afraid he might have been mugged or something—or worse than that."**

**"We'll check with all the local authorities. When are you leaving?"**

**"On Sunday."**

**"Well, that's not much time, but we'll do our best."**

**"And what if he doesn't turn up by then?"**

**"We'll inform you through the proper channels, whatever happens."**

**Outside the embassy, both women paused to settle themselves by a joyous, cascading water fountain surrounded by beggars.**

**"I hate to say that I told you so," Mrs. Covington clucked. "But remember what I said to you about Marvin acting very peculiar these past two days?"**

**"I remember your saying the tux he wore looked like Orson Welles!"**

**"Oh, no," she said, "I had ominous feelings that something like this was going to happen, especially when I noticed he liked to talk to himself."**

**"I've been talking to myself for years," Mrs. Epstein dismissed.**

**"Yes, I know, my dear..." Mrs. Covington dipped her handkerchief into the water fountain and dabbed along her lips and cheek, "...but nobody ever listens to you."**

∞∞

## 6

**Kopfelman dreamed the amnesiac's dream, the tooth hammer drill to unconsciousness in which memory was not lost at all but rudely awakened while sound asleep.**

**"So you had to go on vacation yet to lose your mind..." A man with a beard who looked very much like his grandfather Shlomo was wagging a finger. "There are three generations of rabbis in the family—not counting your father who tripped and fell on his head as a child—and all you do is chase after women in black garter belts and high-heeled shoes."**

**"I wasn't cut out to be a rabbi. I told you before, I'm not very good at languages."**

**"Stop changing the subject. All you do is watch porno movies."**

**"I did it for only kidding around. I was curious."**

**"Yes, for this kind of *drek* you don't need a language, is that what you're saying? Have you any idea what all this means?"**

**In a rush of depression, Kopfelman stared out the window of his grandfather's study and spotted a Puerto Rican woman across the street who was dressed to kill in black pantyhose and high heel boots.**

**"Why must everything have a meaning?" Kopfelman snored. "Logic has nothing to do with this."**

**"You'll end up being buried in logic with all the trimmings," the old man wagged. "A boy with your brains, with so much promise, killing yourself through masturbation!"**

**"I don't want to hear this Talmudic-wisdom-bullshit talk."**

**"There is so much you could do with yourself in other fields. The whole liberal arts curriculum. Take courses in art and philosophy..."**

**"I've been teaching art and philosophy for 16 years and where the fuck did it ever get me? I can't even pay my dental bills."**

**"So maybe you'll take a second job."**

**"I have," he said. "I'm a hit man for the Mafia."**

**"You renounced your faith?"**

**"I never had any faith to begin with."**

**"How could you even talk this way? Are you sick or something? What's the matter? You look run down."**

**"I'm dying of cancer."**

**"God forbid!"**

**Out of nowhere came a crazy woman, tearing her hair out and grabbing at him relentlessly.**

**"*Mein Kindela*, Marvin, what are you saying?"**

"Mother, please, get up off the floor, you're crushing my toes."

"You were never sick a day in your life."

"The kid has been sick since the first day I met him!" Kopfelman's father appeared on cue in a yarmulka with a logo on top that read: New York Mets. "You made him into a fagela, yet—Marvin the Nebbish."

"No, *Marvin the Abruzzi Strangler*!" Kopfelman roared, and severed the spine of his grandfather's desk with a devastating karate chop. "I was born to kill…"

"But Marvin, darling, *oy a broche*, his mother cried. "You haven't had your breakfast yet."

He woke in a fit of perspiration, kicking apart the footboard of the bed, but without remembering anything.

On the dresser was a scotch-taped note from Josephine:

"Called, but you were out like a light. Will give you time to recuperate."

If only he had been awake when she came in the room! He ran the shower and tried to revive while visions of Shalomar danced in his head.

The telephone rang.

"Mr. Zangara, your wake-up call. A woman left a message for you to meet her at The Museum of Fine Arts at twelve o'clock."

"What time is it now?"

"It's ten o'clock."

**"In the morning?"**

**"Yes, of course, senor."**

**He had slept for only a lousy hour or maybe it was the next day's morning?**

**"Yes, senor, today is Sunday. You checked in Friday."**

**One whole day he had slept away! As a matter of fact, he had slept away his entire life since the time he woke with that bump on his head, and the sight of his clothing (the jacket of the suit in the closet ran down to his knuckles) depressed him even more than that, for the one thing that he couldn't explain or understand was why he had failed to have them altered once he knew he had lost so much weight from the onslaught of this ongoing illness—he hated to even think about.**

**He fought off the vagueness surrounding him and gradually focused on details of the room itself, in which everything seemed to look very blurry and far away. Could it be there was something wrong with his eyes? He stumbled over the coffee table one more time and then remembered the money they had left for him in the envelope. There was five grand there in denominations of one thousand dollars, and Kopfelman, who had never seen a thousand dollar bill before (not even in a Monopoly game) could not believe that the money was real, or that anything in this room was real, including himself, so he thrust aside the drapes of the terrace to let in light, and gazed down at the gleaming white beaches, bursting with color and dazzling bodies, bikini-clad bathers daring the surf in the endless vista of surging**

**breakers and hot open sky, baking deeper and deeper and burning into everything...or was it the aura and afterglow of something more intensely alive that made him aware of a missing presence beyond all this, yet so much a part of all of it.**

**He turned away as a tepid sea breeze ruffled the curtains caressingly against his skin, evoking in him the same sensation that Josephine had aroused in him the day before, and which lingered in him relentlessly and restlessly, like some long lost and deluded driver roaring down a one-way street in the wrong direction.**

**Kopfelman picked up the phone inside and felt, somehow, he was on the edge of a precipice with nothing below but his fear of falling. "Room service? Listen. I need a full assortment of clothing: shirts, shoes, ties, the works. I assume you have a men's shop here. You do? Okay..." He was all pumped up and throbbing along the pit of his stomach from not having eaten in...Who knows how long he had gone without food?...and yet, in all this varf and confusion and utter chaos of not knowing what was happening next, he suddenly felt more intensely alive than ever before, and wondered how he could feel this way with six months to live and danger lurking everywhere like a supernova warning light on that catastrophic one-way street. "Yes, send someone up here right away and bring me a pot of coffee and muffins—no make that bagels. Money's no object. Just make it fast."**

**A few hours later, equipped with a wardrobe for two thousand dollars (how easy it was to give away money that didn't really belong to you) and dressed in a white linen three-piece suit (that might very well serve for his burial), he entered the magisterial portals of the *Museo National de Belas Artes* and immediately felt on familiar ground. The paintings, sculptings, objects d'art, even the tourists darting about in total confusion and admiration…maybe he was just kidding himself, or it might have been something like déjà vu, but how could he feel such a deep and abiding security in Degas, Mattise, the abstract impressionists and still find the time to strangle people?**

**Josephine waved and emerged from one of the wings of the lobby, and Kopfelman felt a gastroenteritis attack pursuing him. She was too much for him, and dressed in jeans and a slummy looking sweater-sweatshirt and huge dark glasses that shaded her face theatrically into something very modish and cat-like and carelessly elegant.**

**"Well, don't we look much better today," she eyed him over. "Ready to work?"**

**"Whenever you are," he answered tersely. "Where's your brother, defender of the faith, and why the museum for plotting murder?"**

**As soon as he said it, he realized he was being vindictive, just like the little smart ass clerk who had sold him the suit for nine hundred dollars, yet knew he would never own one himself. The clerk had actually sneered at him when he tried it on, and**

**Kopfelman knew he was sneering at her for want of ever trying her on.**

**"I'm sorry," he said. "That's not what I intended to say. I apologize."**

**"For what?" she smiled. "We don't have to stand on ceremony. You don't have to pick and choose your words."**

**"I know," he said, "but I don't like the way I served them up. That's not my style."**

**Which was what? He thought. What *was* his style when he wasn't all fucked up with amnesia or playing out all these dead ends of unrequited love? He followed her as she strolled through a wing of modern American abstract painters on exhibition.**

**"Carmine is setting the plan in motion, contacting people." She paused before a Paul Klee painting, nodding her head in approbation, lips to the fore, and breathing in the fumes of it, the delicate curve of her nostrils flaring. "Why the museum for plotting murder? That sounds like it should be the title of something." She spoke to the paintings and not to him. "The hotel is tacky, you looked like something the tide washed in, and this is the only place I know where I won't find my brother. Wonderful, isn't it?" This was meant for the painting by Klee. "So full of life and childish mischief. Innocence, really."**

**"You seem to know your art rather well."**

**"An art museum is the only place that makes me feel pure and clean inside."**

**"Do you do any sort of painting yourself?"**

**"Oh, no," she protested. "I'm terrible when it comes to that, but collecting art is my greatest pleasure."**

**"Do you favor any particular trend?"**

**"Such as what?" she asked.**

**"Such as...abstract, hard edge, representational..." Kopfelman felt all the wheels in his head begin to move with unconscious strength and authority. "The Pop-Art fad was not such a failure after all, when you stop to consider the crude burlesque of the world we live in."**

**"Crude burlesque," she repeated softly. "Yes, you're right."**

**"I don't even know what I'm talking about."**

**"Oh, yes you do. I had no idea you were so familiar with all these terms."**

**"I had no idea you collected art."**

**She rolled up her glasses to get a better look at him, she was so impressed.**

**"I have no particular preference when it comes to art. If something strikes me as very special or stirs up some sort of feeling in me that starts to smoke, I'll go out and buy it at any price."**

**"If you know what you're doing, it's usually a very good form of investment."**

**"That's not the reason I do it," she said. "What I want is the thrill of discovery, to find someone new and talented and completely unknown."**

**"You collect unknowns?"**

**"They were all unknown when they started out." She pointed to a painting by Pollack that dwarfed all the other paintings in the room. "Do you sense the power and fury there, the absolute rage and will to live?"**

**"The outrage is unmistakable," he hummed inside, "but to me it still looks like ceiling zero, multiplied by eggdrop soup and splattered linguini."**

**Josephine got a kick out of this.**

**"Where did you learn to talk that way?"**

**"I don't know," he said. "It just seems to keep popping out in me."**

**"There are people who think you're completely deranged and slightly retarded."**

**"They may be right."**

**"No, seriously, they say that when you go into one of your blackout spells…"**

**"What blackout spells?"**

**"You're also epileptic, it seems."**

**"That's beautiful!" Kopfelman reached toward his eyes and adjusted his nose. "Is there anything else that's wrong with me that I don't know about? Does my ass fall off at midnight or something?"**

**Josephine laughed along with him.**

**"You mean, you remember nothing of this?"**

**He shrugged at her and rapidly started losing focus.**

**"What's wrong?" she asked.**

**"I'm getting a headache."**

**"I think you better put on your glasses."**

**"What glasses are you talking about?"**

**"There are two purple marks on the ridge of your nose, and I notice that you've been squinting at me."**

**"I thought it was the glare of the room," he rubbed his eyes.**

**"Do you have them?"**

**"No, I must have lost them while being mugged."**

**"Well, don't you keep an extra pair for emergencies?"**

**He shut his eyes and strained to see if the wheels in his head had anything else to offer him, but all he could picture was reading an eye chart with numbers on it and coming out with alphabet letters.**

**"I really don't remember that much about coming here from…where is that place? Abruzzi, Italy?"**

**"Nunzio."**

**And again he turned ton see who it was she was talking to.**

**"What is it? She said. "You don't look so good."**

**"Let's get out of here and go somewhere. I'm beginning to feel the walls close in."**

**She took him to an outdoor café across the street and lectured him.**

**"I know you're in a weakened condition and obviously not a hundred percent, but there's too much at stake to be careless now."**

**"All right," he said, "I'll go to an optometrist, or maybe I'll get my head examined."**

**"All I want is your eyes examined." Josephine reached out across the way and gripped his hand reassuringly. "I want you with those glasses on and ready to go at a moment's notice."**

**Kopfelman blanched and trembled at this solicitude. Her touch was not only comforting, it also managed to break through the walls of some hidden reserve, something so remote and inhibiting that all he could hear were the wheels inside spinning deeper and deeper to get it out or forever after hold his peace.**

**"Stop me if you've heard this one," he brazened out, yet heard the words rising up in him like the fervent hope of a schoolboy prayer: "For both most need the comrade heart that understands...the touch and warmth of human hands."**

**"Why, Nunzio, that's so lovely," she said. "So beautiful that..." she drew back slowly and carefully pushed his hand aside. "Is that poetry?"**

**"Yes, it must be something I just remembered."**

**"You're really full of surprises today."**

**"If something strikes me as very special or stirs up some sort of feeling in me that starts to smoke..."**

**"Oh, you're terrible."**

**"No, I want you to know that your words are very important to me."**

**"I'll bet they are," she joshed along, though secretly wondering how many "comrade hearts" he had killed with those**

"warm" little deadly hands of his. "Now, let's get down to business here. Let's get serious." She nervously pressed out all the folds on the napkin before her as though it were the gridlock of a battle plan. "The word is out, officially leaked through the grapevine here, that you're looking to meet with Big Al Gavona. Everyone knows you're my father's man, so nobody knows why you've chosen to put the spotlight on yourself, which is why they're going to seek out and find out for themselves."

"You mean they're going to contact me?"

"You can count on having some visitors soon, so don't be surprised and don't say a word to any of them until you meet with the fat man himself."

"Suppose they insist on my talking to them?"

"They know who you are. They won't take any cheap shots here. The important thing is to show them your passport."

"The Mafia leader's cookbook?"

"Yes, the one from father."

"And Carmine likes the frying plan!"

She failed to get the dig he was making.

"The moment they set eyes on that, you shouldn't have any trouble at all convincing them." She then went over the whole thing again. "And if you should ever make it over to Big Al's place…"

"I like the way you stress that 'if'."

"What else can I say? You know the assignment, the risks involved."

**"I was hoping for something more optimistic."**

**"In this line of work there are no guarantees."**

**He agreed with her.**

**"All right," he said. "And if I should be lucky enough to make it there?"**

**"Then you do what only you can do," she winked at him. "That's the beauty part, that you have no need to conceal a weapon."**

**"As Carmine would say, my hands is my weapon, is that what you mean?"**

**Josephine smiled in complete accord and judiciously edged away from him, and Kopfelman, who had all he could do to unzip his fly or lace hi shoes, decided not to conceal this any longer from her and rolled up both the sleeves of his jacket as though preparing a feat of magic or sleight of hand, extending them both for mock inspection.**

**"*Voila*!" he said. "The beauty part. Now you see them, now you don't."**

**She froze as Kopfelman touched her cheek.**

**"It's okay," he said, "I would never dream of harming you. As a matter of fact, to be honest about it…"**

**"I think it's time I better be leaving." She pushed back her chair and called for a check. "I must be going."**

**"Must you?"**

**"Yes."**

**"I was just about to tell you something very important."**

**"My father's expecting a call from me. I have other appointments and things to do."**

**She paid and then got up to leave, and Kopfelman didn't know what to say since he knew he would never see her again and wished she had been just a bit more tactful and less abrupt at saying goodbye.**

**"I guess this is it."**

**"Oh, yes..." she said. "Good luck to you." She nodded stiffly, shaking his hand without so much as a hint or trace that anything they had said to each other had any sort of meaning at all. "Remember, my father depends on you, so I know that you'll never disappoint us..."**

**Kopfelman felt his blood run cold as she threw in a little "even at the cost of your life" and disappeared in the sidewalk crowd behind a poster of "Old Brazil", the solemn weight of her moral injunction and hard-ass departure settling into his shoes and socks like shotgun blasts. He was devastated. He couldn't move, and not only was he unable to move, but where was he moving? How did these people operate? They left you in the middle of nowhere with no way of knowing your left from your right, or where you were going, or what you were supposed to do until somebody found you and possibly put an end to you if they didn't go for the deal you were making, and what he was making (or rather what he had been made for him by Josephine and her lamebrained brother) was so confusing and complicated with cookbooks...and kickbacks...and double agents...and frying**

pans...that he couldn't even remember his name, much less the name of the game he was in, and which kept getting all mixed up in his mind with TV commercials and shopping lists and old-time Ava Gardner movies where every shmuck who ever fell in love with her would always end up getting killed.

*Oy Gevalt*! What a mess he was in!

He sat there in a state of inertia, numbed to the ankles and staring at a crumby looking crippled peddler hobbling on crutches and working the crowd, who for some odd reason unsettled him even more than the parting shotgun blasts from Josephine, or his current state of paralysis. In fact, the more he thought about it, the more he began to realize he had always been a sucker for this passive-submissive bullshit act of waiting on people, and serving people, and hobbling around even worse than he was doing now in this two-dimensional grasshopper world of kill-or-be-killed that had flattened out his entire sense of reality, for he certainly had no wish to die or harm anyone, and what kind of madman would fall in love with a femme fatale to whom it would mean absolutely nothing if weeds started growing out of his ears, and to whom it seemed he was much more preferable dead than alive?

He summoned whatever strength was left and aimlessly wandered the crowded streets and boulevards of midtown Rio, nodding his head like an old Jewish beggar who knows how the world can fuck you this way, and not surprised by a sudden, inexplicable downpour (the sun was shining) that chased him

**under a nearby awning seeking shelter, searching for something to do with himself between here and now and the hotel room, when he noticed the Optometrist sign on the plate-glass window in back of him (like some ineluctable shard of fate that was more than just a coincidence), imagining, as he opened the door, that the gracious old man who greeted him was also prone to Josephine's bidding and priming him for the ultimate sales pitch:**

***"Tell me, my friend, would you rather die with your glasses on, or be buried under a nice little cloud of myopia? Today we have a ten percent discount."***

**Kopfelman paid a thousand dollars for the frame and glasses.**

∞∞

## 7

They had stripped him bare, searched through his clothes and the Gucci bag with the cookbook and the frying pan ("What is this shit?" They hefted the pan. "You can kill a fucking elephant with it.") and packed him into a motor launch with somebody riding shotgun on top and somebody shouting rapid instructions that didn't make sense unless you were good at deciphering grunts and body language. Kopfelman's hands were twisted and tied behind his back.

"Gentlemen, do you really think this is necessary?"

"We just wanna keep those hands out of action."

"Where are we going?"

"It's none of your business."

"It is my business," Kopfelman winced from the crushing rope. "You stripped me naked, roughed me up, and now you've got my blood circulation running up the back of my ass. Is there anything else you forgot to do, like maybe plucking my pubic hairs?"

**"I think we oughta blindfold the fuck and gag his mouth."**

**"All right, okay, boys..." Kopfelman backed down immediately. "Just trying to make polite conversation."**

**"Shut up and don't say a fucking word or we'll shove a two by four up your ass!"**

**Nobody said a word to him for the rest of the trip, and Kopfelman, in the midst of having his fate decided, felt guilty for not having anything to feel guilty about, as ridiculous as he knew that might seem to somebody who was shopping at Waldbaums or having a little root canal work, he mused to himself, for a paradox was the last thing that he needed right now, especially one that was not your average blue collar existential question of having to buy a six-pack of beer or beat your wife, but a question of who would care for him, or mourn for him, or hate him enough to have earned the right to make him feel guilty!**

**Kopfelman pondered long and hard and peered about the gathering dusk of his isolation, wondering how the end would come and trying to dredge up some sort of feeling for his wife and kids back in Italy, though he couldn't even recall their names or remember enough to speak the language. All he could manage to conjure up was "Fresco, al dente, and no parmigiana." That was the thing he couldn't quite figure out to himself, for how could he forget his Italian, his own native language, yet still remember having stolen a peanut brittle from Julie's drugstore—wherever that was!**

**"Does anyone have a piece of candy? I haven't had a thing to eat."**

**"Then suck on your dick."**

**"You know, you have a filthy mouth."**

**"Go fuck yourself!"**

**"Do you know any words that begin with S?"**

**"Why, do you think you're so tough we're scared of you?"**

**"I didn't come here to start any trouble."**

**"Yeah, look who's talking, the guy who would kill his own fucking mother to make a hit."**

**Kopfelman strained to remember his mother, but all that emerged was the blurry picture of someone chasing after him with a hot water bottle and black syringe.**

**"Does anyone know a prayer for the dead?"**

**"You better not try no shit with us, you little Zulu motherfucker!"**

**When the boat disembarked, he was hustled into a limousine by two other men in combat clothes, and searched again.**

**"Is this the guy?"**

**"Yeah, this is the Abruzzi Strangler."**

**"Go ahead."**

**They traveled along an unpaved road that was flanked by towering barbed wire fences, and every so often the drive was stopped as armed guards checked for identification.**

**"If you think it's hard getting into this place," the driver joked, "you oughta try getting outta here!"**

**He swerved through the gate of a sprawling compound, a self-enclosed world of everything you would expect to find in a thriving suburban community, including a golf course and tennis courts, and an airstrip replete with the two Lear jets and a helicopter. The only thing missing was a supermarket.**

**"We even got a church over here," the driver boasted solemnly. "The boss is very religious, you know."**

**He crossed himself and eased along a circular ramp to the entranceway of a three-story mansion that looked like a high camp advertisement for architectural plastic surgery. Kopfelman counted six different styles, not the least of which was "Early Bronx" and something that maybe Frank Lloyd Wright might have tried to conceive under LSD.**

**The driver withdrew a plastic disc and plugged it into a slot in the door.**

**"We're computerized," he explained to Kopfelman. "Everything here is state of the art."**

**"You could put me in a state of relief by untying me."**

**They released his hands and led him into a dimly lighted, circular room with red-flocked walls and chromium-accented furniture. It was obviously meant to look like a nightclub, Art-Deco style, with tables, booths, a rather extensive drape-covered stage, and a full-length bar that snaked along the contours of the room like an orbiting moon ring.**

**"You wanna drink? The boss is probably busy right now."**

**He driver became the bartender now while the other two men sat quietly with their guns exposed.**

**"Do you have a candy?"**

**"You're not gonna find no candy here. The boss weighs over five hundred pounds and he ain't allowed to have no sweets. It's strictly off limits. Doctor's orders. Don't even bring it up again 'cause he gets too excited. He once ate six pounds of Halvah before dessert—just for openers."**

**The other two men were snickering despite themselves and Kopfelman felt a bit more relaxed.**

**"Do you have any coke?"**

**"What kind you want?"**

**"Any kind you have, as long as it's cold."**

**"You want it *cold*?"**

**"If you have it, yeah."**

**The driver gave him a fishy look. "That's a new one on me." He drew out a metal tray from the bar and spread a liberal dosage of powder in thin white strips that he then proceeded to snort through his nose with the help of a straw. "I ain't got the time to chill this shit, but believe me, you ain't gonna get any better anywhere—and that goes for Don Vincenzo and his fucking Chinks!"**

**He passed the straw to Kopfelman, who had no idea what was going on.**

**"What is this stuff?"**

**"Our name for it here is Antilles One. We're jacking it out at two mil a kilo and that's undercutting everyone. You can't get it nowhere else in the States for that kind of money."**

**Politely, Kopfelman passed back the straw.**

**"I'm sorry," he said, "but all I wanted was...Coca Cola."**

**"Coca Cola?" The driver repeated, then stared at the other two men in the room and they burst out laughing hysterically.**

**"I'm thirsty," Kopfelman laughed along.**

**"...he's thirsty..."**

**"...he's a *brutto scifuso*..."**

**"...forget about it!..."**

**Kopfelman didn't know what he was saying that seemed to hit off so humorously, but each new attempt at explaining himself was enough to provoke a new wave of laughter.**

**"All right," he smiled, "I'll settle for water."**

**"...he'll settle for *water*..."**

**The driver and the other two men were down on their knees and shaking all over helplessly when the boss appeared.**

**"What the hell's going on over here? What's so funny?"**

**"Our friend here is a comedian." The driver wiped a tear away. "He put us on by asking for coke, then said what he meant was Coca Cola."**

**Big Al smiled appreciatively. He was maybe two or three inches away from being installed in a temple in China, and so grotesquely Buddha-like, so interlarded with double chins and**

**layers of fat, that Kopfelman didn't know how in the world he was ever going to strangle him.**

**"It was something I thought of to break up the tension," Kopfelman fell right in with them and was smiling such a cowardly smile of ingratiation, his teeth were aching. "After all, when a man decides to risk his life to tell you that he's been hired to kill you by your own worst enemy, what has he got to lose by laughing?"**

**The fat man sat in a throne-like chair that was wheeled out to him and studied Kopfelman carefully. He was swaddled in a dark silk robe that squished through every pore of his being, every move he made, like an out-of-kilter waterbed that had now assumed a life of its own.**

**"That's all well and good, but why did you turn against Don Vincenzo and come to me with this *ingannare*—this double cross?"**

**"That's a very good question," Kopfelman stalled, and one for which a warning voice cried out to him: Marvin, go home, your nose is bleeding! "I know it must look very bad for me, like maybe I'm trying to pull a fast one, and God only knows you have every right to be suspicious..." He turned and saw the other men staring straight through his eyes and into his brain. "...but believe me, it's very complicated..." So complicated, he couldn't remember a single word that Josephine had spoken to him about what he was supposed to say, and now he was up to his neck in shit and pictured himself with cattle prods being shoved up his ass**

**to make him talk, if he didn't start getting his act together immediately.**

**"What's the matter?"**

**"Nothing," he said. "I just want to put this right to you, so you'll understand my predicament."**

**"Look, let's cut out all the bullshit talk. You came out here with a contract on me, and I wanna know why you're switching sides."**

**"Double indemnity."**

**"What the fuck are you talking about?"**

**Kopfelman swallowed uneasily and improvised on a sliding scale of panic and fear.**

**"It doesn't exactly take a genius to figure out that trying to make a hit on you in a place like this is impossible, so I figured I would take the money from Don Vincenzo, go through the motions of getting to you, and once I'm here..." He searched about for the nearest exit. "I warn you about the danger you're in."**

**"And whatta you want, a fucking medal?"**

**"I thought we could maybe do business together."**

**"What kind've business?"**

**"Staying alive business."**

**Big Al laughed derisively.**

**"You're funny, all right. You ain't worth fucking shit to me."**

**"I know," he said, "but..." Kopfelman spied the Gucci bag. "To show good faith, I brought along a few little things that might**

**be worth two shits to you!" He motioned to the men in the room. "Would you gentlemen please show Mr. Gavona the stuff you took away from me?"**

**They brought Big Al the Gucci bag with the cookbook and the frying pan.**

**"What is this shit?"**

**"The one thing that you've always been after and never could get," Kopfelman proffered. "Don Vincenzo's frying pan and his own secret cookbook of recipes from your mob days together."**

**Big Al choked and grew so excited his blimp-like face had begun to expand exponentially into something indescribably lewd and pornographic.**

**"That sonofabitch!" He trembled with the book in his hand. "I can't believe how you got this thing."**

**"Well, the moment I knew that I wasn't going to make the hit and get killed for it, I decided I needed some short-term insurance."**

**"I'll give you insurance," the fat man scoffed sarcastically. "This better be the real thing, kid, or I'll hang you up by the fucking balls and cut off your dick for openers!"**

**He plunged through the book and riffled the pages.**

**"Yeah…yeah…yeah…this is Don Vincenzo's writing alright, the faggart cocksucker." Spittle drooled and slobbered along the side of his mouth as he burrowed even deeper in the book. "AHA…AHA…" He stumbled up to rise from his chair and awkwardly fell to his knees on the floor, as though he were having**

**a heart attack. "The risotto," he choked. "I should've known after all these years..." He shook his fist at the page he was reading and wildly flailed at two of his men who had rushed to support him. "That *Palermotane* motherfucker put nutmeg in the Risotto Milanese!"**

**"All right, boss, come on, sit down. You know what the doctors said to you about getting excited."**

**"...and look at this! He put Chinese shit in the calamari, that little rat fuck organ grinder."**

**Big Al gasped and lost his breath, and when nobody knew what to do about it, Kopfelman rushed to the stricken figure and pushed aside all the bodyguards. "Get him some water, the man is dying, just don't stand there."**

**Everyone ran off in different directions, and Kopfelman (who was all alone with the fat man's body slobbering by the foot of the couch and helplessly ripe for execution) could not have had a more perfect setup for doing what he'd been sent here to do, and paid to do, and that untold years of strangling people had trained him to do with such brutal dispatch and efficiency, but instead of grabbing at Big Al's throat to finish him off and give it the old Abruzzi touch, he reached instead for the edge of the couch and gripped his stomach, belching and farting and dropping down to his knees on the floor alongside his intended victim.**

***"Get up, you schmuck, before they come back and see what you're doing."***

**"I'm not doing anything," Kopfelman moaned. "I'm having a violent gas attack."**

**"This is not the place for constipation."**

**"I know," he said. "This whole thing is wrong."**

**"It's not only wrong, it isn't Kosher?"**

**"You think he gives a shit about *Kosher*?"**

**"A fat man deserves to die in peace like everyone else."**

**"He's a madman."**

**"Yes, and ten minutes with these *Italyanisha*—just take a look at what's doing with you."**

**He took a look and stared at himself in the chrome-based lamp across the way as though somebody else were spying on him from another world...a boy with knickers...angry because his nose wasn't broken like all the other neighborhood bums who were getting laid to beat the band...and in the ensuing, bumbling confusion of splotchy-textured video footage that raced through his mind, a sickening thud kicked upward from the base of his brain into consciousness that his name was Marvin Kopfelman!**

***"...Marvin...please...a boy with your brains...with so much promise...killing yourself through masturbation..."***

**Where had he heard that voice before?**

**He tried getting up, but try as he might to sift through the wreckage and dismembered pieces of who he was or who he wasn't, all he remembered before being mugged was fear of flying, somebody choking the shit out of him named Ida**

**Blavatnick, and going for a midnight stroll that turned out to be a total disaster.**

**The rest was still unclear to him, except for the fact that he wasn't who they thought he was, and maybe he wasn't dying of cancer and didn't have any wife and kids back in Italy—or any other of that mishegas that had dug a hole so deep for him, he would probably end up buried in it.**

**By the time the men had returned with the water and smelling salts, Kopfelman had revived Big Al by accidentally stepping on the fat man's toes while trying to wrestle the cookbook out from under his ass, so it wouldn't be damaged. His life preserver.**

**"It's all right," he said for the benefit of all to hear, including Al, "I managed to bring him back by myself with some mouth-to-mouth resuscitation." He took the water and guided Big Al's mouth to the glass like a mother hen. "You feel any better?"**

**"Hey, boss, you want the smelling salts?" The driver asked.**

**"No, give them to me when I wake up again, you stupid bastard! Go get my pills and a glass of wine."**

**He spit out the water and gradually, as he came to himself, his color restored to a talcum-powdered off-putrid white.**

**"Zangara, you did good for yourself. You did good to bring the book to me. I like your balls." He swilled down the wine and some heart medication the driver had brought him. "And better than that, I like the fact you got six months to live, you no good, scheming, lowlife cocksucker, so here's what I'm gonna do with**

**you. I'm gonna give you a fucking chance to prove yourself and really earn your double indemnity bullshit talk."**

**"Tony, get the nigger in the kitchen to make up some Risotto Milanese from Don Vincenzo's recipe book."**

**"Do you want him to use the frying pan?"**

**"Of course you use the frying pan, you fucking moron, whatta you think he risked his life to bring it here for, so guys like you can shit in it? Now get outta here and tell him I wanna eat right away—and whatever you do, don't wash the pan! I'll take care of it.**

**"These guys don't know their ass from their elbow when it comes to food." He poured out another glass of wine and offered it to Kopfelman. "This is better than Coca Cola, kid. Are you on any special medication for the shit you got?"**

**Kopfelman gave him his glummest look. "No, it's too late for that, and besides, it wouldn't do any good."**

**"Well, here's to Don Vincenzo," he toasted. "I want you to go back to New York and get that Chink-loving sonofabitch, and whack him out."**

**Kopfelman saw the hole getting deeper. "How could I do a thing like that when he knows, by now, he's been double-crossed?"**

**"But he *don't* know!" Big Al winked at him. "And he's not gonna know."**

**"I don't understand."**

**"Well, *sta'tasita*, shut up and listen. I got an idea that's gonna be good for both of us: You get the money and I get revenge."**

**He would fake his death and plant stories of his assassination in all the papers. Then when it got back to the States that Big Al had been strangled to death, and that Nunzio, the Abruzzi Strangler, had managed to escape with his life, he would not only live to collect the extra money involved for doing the job, but would also return as Don Vincenzo's conquering hero.**

**"The guy is liable to give you a blow job," one of the bodyguards jabbed at him.**

**"He'll be so relaxed and off his guard at the news of my death that he won't know what hit him when you rip his head off." Big Al grew excited again at this master stroke of Machiavellian double dealing.**

**"You do this for me and I'll match whatever that scumbag gave you to do me in, and then who the fuck is better than you? You're getting paid twice—for the hit you never made on me and the hit you're gonna make on him—which believe me, kid, is so complicated I can't even take the credit for it," the fat man waved off modestly. "The only way it could've worked out is by accident, which is really what I like about it, the accident part, 'cause it's almost like an act of fate that this prick should die in the hands of the man he hired to kill me!"**

**Kopfelman thought he detected a light at the top of the hole he had dug for himself.**

**"That's also what's known as irony."**

**"You bet your ass he'll be ironed out, that no good fucking *brutto schiffuso*!"**

**"Listen, boss..." the driver intruded hesitantly, "I don't wanna get you upset or nothing, but what if our friend here skips with the money and don't do the job?"**

**The fat man squished uncomfortably.**

**"Why, you didn't think I thought of that?"**

**"Well, I only thought that..."**

**"Shut up," he said. "You stupid fuck. The last time you had a thought in your head, you was doing time in Alcatraz!."**

**"I'm sorry, boss. I..."**

**"Where the fuck was I"**

**"Making sure I kill Don Vincenzo," Kopfelman answered.**

**"That's right, sure...you get three days grace to do the job, tie up whatever loose ends you want with your family and stuff, and then if you try to skip with the money and don't do the job," he punctuated, "we let it be known that I'm still alive!" He delivered this with the unmistakable mark of genius showing in every wart and blemish and molehair of his fat sweaty face. "And whatta you think your life will be worth when Don Vincenzo finds out about it—especially when I call to tell him you're working for me?"**

**Another little ingenious twist that brought a cheer from the rooting section and seemed to satisfy everyone there, and to Kopfelman, who was still struck dumb by this unexpected turn of events, it was more than just a brief reprieve, it was so much like**

a miracle of total salvation, he secretly vowed to do charity work for the rest of his life and kiss the feet of itinerant beggars and pregnant women if only they would be stupid enough to let him off this island alive, which could also be a trap they were setting. Some devious way of testing him.

"I would never take the money and run," he lied to them. "And as far as Don Vincenzo is concerned, what makes you think I would risk going back after selling him out to come over here?'

"As far as Don Vincenzo's concerned," Big Al repeated sarcastically, "you came over here to knock me off and that's what you did, so nobody knows you sold him out. That's bullshit talk."

"Look, all I have is six months to live, and I don't want to spend it getting killed."

"You won't get killed, it's the easiest fucking setup in the world."

"Believe me, I have no more stomach for this kind of business."

"All it takes is a little balls."

"I feel safer here."

"You wanna spend your last days here and rot away like a vegetable, you're perfectly welcome," Big Al edged impatiently, "but you ain't ever gonna leave this place as long as Don Vincenzo's alive and you're alive."

"I can't even take a trip to the mainland?"

**"You can't even take a shit around here unless you have my fucking permission and check it out."**

**"I don't seem to have much choice in the matter."**

**"You got the choice of a lifetime, kid!" The fat man conned him passionately. "You take out the Don when nobody's looking, and then you let them chase you around the rest of the world with a fucking million bucks up your gool, and who the fuck is better than you?"**

**Kopfelman feigned a shrug of reluctance and shook his head.**

**"I guess you win."**

**"We all come out winners the moment that fucking bum is dead."**

**"You drive a very hard bargain, Mr. Gavona."**

**"Just call me Al," the fat man beamed.**

ooo

# 8

Dinner was served in a gym-sized room that looked like a set for Citizen Kane, austerely lit and decorated with all the élan of a shopping mall, but also with paintings that must have cost a considerable fortune if any of them were originals.

"The hand of fate," Big Al repeated, going over the same ground again and dishing out heaps of antipasto.

Kopfelman broke some bread with the boys who were friendlier now and more at ease. "You're looking for poetic justice, and all I want is a place to sleep."

"Taste the risotto, put more calamari on your plate, you look like a fucking skeleton with your peace and quiet bullshit stories."

"You know who he looks like?" One of the bodyguards shook his head and burst out laughing. "That little guy that acts in the movies and always wears glasses. What's his name? I can't remember. The one who's always getting in trouble and always getting fucked up with women..." He turned and winked at Kopfelman. "I hope you don't get insulted or nothing, like some

**people say I look like someone I don't even think I look like, you know?"**

**"I don't even know who you're talking about."**

**"Forget who the fuck he's talking about." Big Al shoveled spoon after spoon of food in his mouth at ground level zero, surfacing only now and then to come up for air and further his plans with Kopfelman, then burrowing into the plate again, his words almost indistinguishable from the sounds that he made in combat with the food, as though he were in a private war of *belle cuisine* in which no one took any prisoners. "We can get you back to New York from here. We can fly you out tomorrow night."**

**"Are you serious?'**

**"Yes, of course I'm serious. Why waste time?"**

**Kopfelman played with the food on his plate and sipped more wine than was good for him.**

**"Where can you get that kind of money in twenty-four hours?"**

**"That's not your problem."**

**"It has to be...negotiable cash."**

**"The fucking money's clean as a whistle."**

**"Just how much are we talking about?"**

**"Well, you mentioned half a million bucks from Don Vincenzo to take me out, so the least I could do is match it, right?"**

**"I don't know," Kopfelman hesitated. The whole proposition was so absurdly staggering, he could feel the corruption crawling**

**at him from Big Al's plate like an undigested piece of squid. "How do I get all that money through customs?"**

**"Connections, Nunzio, how do you think we manage to survive? We have customs agents all over the world. At Kennedy Airport you go through customs gate A-18 and the guy will pass you right on through after looking through all your underwear."**

**For that kind of money, a man with amnesia could well afford to sell out whatever part of himself was still intact and start his life all over again, and not only that! But what if he disappeared with the money and never reported to Don Vincenzo or anyone else? How could they ever get back at him or track him down—if he wasn't who they thought he was?**

**He was so overwhelmed by the obvious flaw in Big Al's plan that all he could think of was running as far and as fast as he could while the going was good, and they'd even provide the transportation, these geniuses. That was the kicker. That was the one thing that Josephine never…**

**How could he leave without Josephine?**

**How would he ever see her again if he just took off and disappeared and never said goodbye to her, or at least let her know he was still alive? She probably thought he was dead by now, or didn't care, or whatever she thought or didn't think—and no matter how insane it was, he considered coldly, he knew he had to see her again just one more time and explain the whole situation to her.**

**"Hey, Nunzio, are you all right there? You look like maybe you seen a ghost."**

**"I'm thinking."**

**"Yeah? Well, don't take too long."**

**Kopfelman got up and paced the room, pretending he was checking the paintings (and finding one hanging upside down) but thinking only of Josephine and struggling against the sinking sensation of knowing how little sense it made, how much of a hopeless case he was, to go to the enemy seeking love.**

**"All right," he said.**

**"You'll do it?"**

**"Yes, but I have to go back to my hotel room and get some things."**

**"Why, whatta you need there you can't get here?"**

**"I forgot to bring my passport along. I left it in the hotel safe, just in case I wasn't coming back."**

**"We'll get it for you."**

**"I appreciate all your helpfulness, but I'm the only one who can get it. Those were the instructions I left."**

**"I think he's got a cunt back there," the driver teased.**

**"We got everything you want over here," Big Al grunted, stuffing his mouth with Chicken a la Tetrazada." You wanna get laid, we get you laid. I own this whole fucking island here and every elected official in Rio. How much do you think I'm worth?"**

**"I'm sure it's a lot."**

**"You bet your ass! I been helping pay off the national debt of this whole fucking country," Big Al licked at his fingertips. "Half of the soldiers you see around here are part of their army, but work for me, 'cause they know what that white stuff can do for them."**

**"I assume you don't have to pay any taxes."**

**Big Al nodded appreciatively.**

**"Just look at all the paintings I got."**

**"I've been noticing them."**

**"My social security."**

**"Reproductions?"**

**"Your cock has reproductions, my friend, these paintings are all originals."**

**"The boss is really good at this stuff," the driver threw in obsequiously. "He's getting to be pretty famous about it."**

**"But sometimes people can fool you too," the fat man cranked up his eye a notch at Kopfelman. "Some guy I knew, who really owed me, brought me over a famous painting by Velazquez that didn't check out and turned out to be an imitation, that no-good dirty douche-bag cunt, and that was the first time I ever got a heart attack."**

**"We killed him, boss, so don't let it get you upset no more."**

**"Shut up, you prick! We didn't kill him. What the fuck are you talking about? The guy got into an accident."**

**"Yeah, he opened the door and his house blew up."**

**"You don't talk that way in front of strangers!" Big Al warned. "I like a joke as good as the next guy, but not when it comes to family business."**

**"I thought he was part of the family, boss."**

**"We'll see about that."**

**Big Al rose uncomfortably and neatly wiped at the corners of his mouth while the back of his robe clung moistly to the buttline of his humongous behind.**

**"You know Picasso?" He suddenly turned on Kopfelman. "You know they stole a painting of his from a museum in Paris, worth six million dollars?"**

**"That's quite a theft."**

**"Well, who do you think owns that painting now?"**

**"You own a Picasso?"**

**"It's in the vault," he mopped his face. He was leaking sweat from every pore. "We still haven't found a...What the fuck happened to the air conditioning? Turn it up, you cheap cocksucker!" He shouted inside.**

**The cook appeared in the entranceway.**

**"But, boss, we're wasting electricity."**

**"Stop saving me money and get back inside and get the dessert. Now...what was I saying?"**

**"It's in the vault."**

**"Yeah, we still haven't found a place to hang it."**

**Kopfelman studied the wall arrangement and quickly conceived a realignment if one of the other paintings were moved to make place for it.**

**"Why not move the portrait of your mother…"**

**"That's not my mother, that's me, you fuck!"**

**The men at the table had all they could do to restrain themselves.**

**"I'm sorry…I meant if you moved that painting, then maybe you could place the Picasso by the Mondrian."**

**"How did you know that was Mondrian?" Big Al asked suspiciously. "I got very smart friends who don't even know who the fuck he is."**

**Kopfelman couldn't believe his blunder. *Marvin* was going to get him killed if *Nunzio* didn't come to the rescue.**

**"Hey, what the fuck do you want from me? The painting was hanging upside down, so I thought I'd look at the painter's name…to see if the name was upside down."**

**Big Al rushed to examine the painting.**

**"How did you know it was upside down?"**

**"Why, you think I'm retarded?" Kopfelman snapped indignantly. "You think all I do is kill for a living? You think I got no culture in me?"**

**"That's not what I said."**

**"You think we Italians don't know these things about Art and Opera and all that shit, without being told or having to go to school for it? You don't think that it's in our blood?"**

**"You're goddamn right it's in our blood!" Big Al's nose flared imperiously. "Who's arguing?" He turned to see which one of his men has been dumb enough to start all this. "You stupid fucks, you can't even hang a picture up right?"**

**"But you're the one who hung it, boss..." the driver squeaked.**

**"Shut up, you prick, I'm talking to him." He threw an arm around Kopfelman. "So whatta you think?"**

**"About Mondrian?"**

**"No, my art collection. All the stuff you see around here."**

**Kopfelman batted a lazy eye.**

**"You have paintings here that most museums would love to have for just one exhibition." He got up and walked across the room to give the paintings a better look. "If you want to, you can use some better lighting in here to cut down some of the glare effect."**

**"Those fucking Chicano lowlife bastards!" Big Al played with the light switch a moment. "They screwed up all the wiring here and then they talk about revolution and communism, those *moolenyan*! He opened a box of special imported Cuban cigars. "When Castro stops fucking ten year old girls, their economy's gonna fold up and die." He lit one up and offered one to Kopfelman. "If you wanna go back to your fucking hotel and get your passport, Rinzi will take you."**

**"Who's Rinzi?"**

**"My driver."**

**"I gave him the guided tour around here," Rinzi acknowledged, and Kopfelman had to think hard and fast to get a little breathing room.**

**"There's another thing I neglected to mention…a special lady I have to say goodbye to here."**

**"I told you there was a cunt involved." The driver boomed.**

**"It's not for discussion," Kopfelman answered.**

**"Listen, kid, I don't want any fuckups here. I don't want you mixing business with pleasure," Big Al counseled. "Just do whatever you gotta do and I want you back by tomorrow noon. Get rid of the broad!"**

ꝏꝏ

**Two hours later, Rinzi dropped off Kopfelman at the hotel La Condessa del Mar and briefed him as to departure time.**

**"The boat will pick you up tomorrow at two o'clock, so give her a fucking good one for me, and you better be ready!"**

**"I'll be ready when the money is ready."**

**"The money ain't no problem, *strunz,* so just make sure that you ain't the problem!"**

**Kopfelman watched the car depart, then sprinted through the hotel lobby, screeching to a halt by the desk where Carmine was seated.**

**"Well, well, well…will you look who's here," Carmine greeted, folding away the newspaper he was pretending to read**

**and rising from a plush, leather armchair, nice and easy. "Just the man I been waiting for."**

**"I didn't think I was coming back, there's a change of plans."**

**"I'll say there's been a change in plans, you cross-eyed fuck!"**

**But Kopfelman failed to get the drift of Carmine's hulking presence there.**

**"Look, I don't have time to argue about it, I'm in a rush. If you want to talk, let's go to my room."**

**"That's just the point, you ain't got no room. Two hours ago the police came here and removed all your clothing and personal possessions."**

**"The police?"**

**"That's right, the fucking police, and because I'm a very friendly guy, I asked them what was going on, and you know what they told me?" Carmine chuckled menacingly. "They told me that you drowned about a day ago."**

**Kopfelman hadn't the vaguest idea what was going on. His brain was awhirl.**

**"It must be some sort of stupid mistake."**

**"No, you're the one who's stupid, my friend, because Nunzio Zangara is dead—and they found the registration receipt for this hotel in his passport papers!"**

**All the pieces clicked into place with a shattering jolt.**

**"The room key..." Kopfelman blurted out. "I picked it up and...Oh, my God!"**

**"Yeah, you better say your prayers, you fuck."**

**"All kidding aside, this whole thing was a big mistake, and I didn't have to come back here, you know. I could have just disappeared on you."**

**"So what're you saying"**

**I'm saying I'm not the Abruzzi Strangler."**

**"*You're probably not even Italian*, you prick!"**

**"Would you lower your voice, there are people staring."**

**"Then who the fuck are you?" Carmine challenged.**

**"I wish I knew…"**

**"Well, you won't have to wish for very long." A gun slid out from under the paper and jammed itself into Kopfelman's crotch. "If Big Al Gavona's still alive, you're a dead man, pal."**

∞∞

# 9

**In a private suite, not far from the one that was sealed off by the local police, Carmine was practicing ancient history on Kopfelman's head and sweating him with interrogation, when Josephine came crashing in like a woman possessed and started flinging things around in a distillation of wild-eyed fury, slamming doors, and acting as though her darkest, deepest, most personal sexual fantasies had somehow been secretly microfilmed and offered up for publication.**

**"What are you doing?"**

**"I'm trying to help his memory along."**

**"That's not the way to handle this," she snapped at him. "That won't accomplish a goddamn thing."**

**"Then whatta you want me to do with him, massage his ass?"**

**"Just leave us alone and go downstairs and watch the lobby, see if anyone followed him here."**

**Carmine submitted reluctantly.**

**"The guy's a creep. He may be a plant."**

**"He may also be an undercover agent," Josephine warned. "That's all we need is the CIA on top of us."**

**"Well, don't take any chances with him."**

**"I'll be all right, just leave things to me."**

**"The fucking guy gives me *agita.*"**

**"Will you go downstairs? If I need you, I'll call you."**

**Carmine lumbered out of the room.**

**"I think we oughta get rid of the prick before it's too late."**

**"All right," she said. "You made your point."**

**As soon as he left, she turned on Kopfelman viciously.**

**"You better start talking and make some sense."**

**"I didn't have to come back here, you know."**

**"Come back from where? Did you ever even contact them?"**

**"Of course I did. They think that I'm the Abruzzi Strangler."**

**"I don't understand what's going on. You mean you were there and they let you go?"**

**"I did everything that you told me to do, except...that I couldn't kill anybody, and that's when I knew that I wasn't who I thought I was."**

**"Who are you then?"**

**"I told your brother, I really don't know."**

**"Then how on earth did you ever get in the Strangler's room?"**

**"I found a key on the beach somewhere and..."**

**"Don't tell me that you picked it up?"**

**"I was mugged," he had to remind her again. "I didn't know where the hell I was or what I was doing. I told you, I lost memory."**

**"You may also have lost your stupid life. The word from New York is get rid of you!"**

**"Why?"**

**"You know too much."**

**"But the enemies of your father don't know, and they offered me a half million dollars to knock him off."**

**"I knew there was something wrong with you the minute I laid eyes on you," she cursed herself, for when Carmine was right, the whole world was wrong. "Do you really think I believe that shit?"**

**"I only ask that you listen to me."**

**"Oh, come on, will you, what's your game?"**

**"I don't have a game. You don't even know the half of it."**

**"This is absolutely ridiculous."**

**"No, listen to me, the whole thing gets more complicated, I don't feel so good. I've been eating Italian food all day."**

**"The cookbook?"**

**"Yes, the one you gave me to give to Big Al."**

**"He went for it?"**

**"He was out of his mind with ecstasy over it. Everyone bought the whole idea of my going against your father with them."**

**"Then they have no way of knowing who you are?"**

**"I've been trying to get that across to you for the past five minutes." Kopfelman reached for a cigarette and coughed when he tried to light it up.**

**"What am I doing, I don't even smoke."**

**"Here, give it to me."**

**"They want me to get rid of your father by faking that I made the hit and succeeded in escaping from them." He explained their entire scheme to her in intricate detail. "Big Al's death would then appear in all the papers, and Don Vincenzo would welcome me with open arms as the conquering hero, which would make your father a sitting duck for whatever I'd want to do to him, which naturally I would never do."**

**She inhaled deeply, mulling it over.**

**"You have the money?"**

**"Tomorrow noon. They have me on a flight to New York, and they don't even know who the hell I am any more than I do."**

**Josephine thought she had met them all, but none like this.**

**"In other words, you could easily have taken the money and run…and no one would ever have known the difference?"**

**"I could have done that, sure," he said, "but I just couldn't leave without seeing you."**

**"What does seeing me have to do with it? You're not making sense."**

**"That's part of the problem," Kopfelman tried to portion out. "I think that I'm in love with you…"**

**"In *love* with me?" She reeled back a step to catch her breath. "Have you any idea what you're talking about?"**

**He knew he had blundered and leaned forward with his knees together, as though bailing out of the open hatch of an airplane and finding out his rip cord was missing, or that somehow he had landed in Afghanistan.**

**"I'm sorry," he apologized. "I know this must sound like a joke to you." He made quick amends by removing his glasses and placing them on the floor by his feet as she sat down across the way from him and stared at him, her sleek, cutting features losing composure and thinning into merciful blurs of cigarette smoke. "But you wanted to know, and I just had to get it out of me before leaving here and maybe never seeing you again. I didn't mean to embarrass you."**

**"I'm not embarrassed," her voice rose up defensively. "Just deeply surprised." She glanced in the mirror in back of him and wondered what, in that poor dismembered mind of his, he could possibly even see in her? She was flat-chested, beat and bedraggled looking, and more like a zombie than ever before. "I mean, please try to understand, if you will," she edged at him sarcastically, "it's not every day that a man you hardly know at all risks life and limb to place himself on the line for you, and ends up with a ten gun salute to undying love."**

**"You make it sound very patriotic."**

**"Is that what I'm doing?"**

**"I suddenly feel like saluting the flag."**

**She had no idea where the landscape began and ended with him. Was he serious? Was he putting her on? He had nothing to gain in either respect.**

**"You talk as if you somehow expect me to read your mind."**

**"I would settle for something less comforting, like a slap in the face to let me know I have your attention."**

**She poured out a glass of Scotch for herself and plopped down into an easy chair. He was out of it. He was off the wall. She had never heard such nonsense before, and yet, she thought...there was something about the astounding range of his naiveté and offbeat remarks that appealed to her in a way she could not define to herself, any more than she could her being out here and doing her father's dirty work.**

**"You have my attention."**

**"I want you to be honest with me."**

**"All right," she said. "I've had men who said they loved me before, but never under such circumstances."**

**"What kind of men?"**

**"Just men who were after my father's name and using me as a way to strengthen their own position." She glanced down to gauge the effect on him. "Not unusual for a Mafia leader's daughter, you know, and you don't have to be a beauty either. That's the part that always upset me. These marvelous looking, sleek-haired men with muscles and shoulders and women chasing after them that you weren't supposed to know about, and so easy to see through, it always made me want to puke." She brushed by**

**his elbow and watched him freeze at the touch of her. "Not men who would risk their life for you!" She underscored with a slight mocking edge that she couldn't resist or repress in herself after years and years of self-denial and having been exploited this way. "I mean, no one in my entire life has ever shown me that kind of love, and believe me—I am deeply touched, and those men couldn't hold a candle to you...but this isn't the proper time or place, and we hardly even know each other."**

**Know each other? Kopfelman felt the cutting edge of Josephine's words as though it were a ritual form of his own impalement rising up like a stake through his heart, for the irony was he had dreamed about her all his life, the way Big Al dreamed about getting revenge on Don Vincenzo, while stuffing his mouth with Halvah.**

**"Who has to know," he fumbled out, "when all you have to do is feel?"**

**She responded to this by nervously pinning her hair back straight, and with no apparent connection at all—in the measureless distance separating Kopfelman's words from anything he had meant to arouse or evoke in her—was reminded of her Catholic school days, when boys who had offered to take her to the prom had later reneged when they found out who her father was.**

**"I like that very much," she said. "Is that poetry?"**

**"No, the last time was poetry," Kopfelman reminded her. "You remember the last time you said that to me?"**

**She didn't remember.**

**"Across the street from the museum we went to, that outdoor café..."**

**"Oh, yes," she said. *"The touch and warmth of human hands."***

**"That's right," he said, "and then when we touched, you got up and left and got rid of me like I had the plague. The kiss of death."**

**"I had no idea you were harmless then. I was frightened of you. I thought you were the Abruzzi Strangler."**

**"In other words, you were playing along just to humor me."**

**"You were going to kill somebody and never come back, so what was I supposed to do, get involved with you?"**

**"No...hearts and flowers I didn't expect," he leveled at her seriously, "but the act you put on was so convincing, you almost had me believing you."**

**"That's part of the business," Josephine stiffened. "That's what I'm here for."**

**"Okay," he said. "I can live with that."**

**"No. I don't think you want to live with that!" she zinged at him. "You want me to apologize? Is that what you want?"**

**"I'm sorry," he said. "I was out of line."**

**"No, you're right on line, and you know it."**

**"Look..."**

**She was furious at the thought of having been challenged this way, of having been stripped of all her clothes by a total stranger.**

**"I guess you must think I'm some heartless little bimbo bitch who sends men off to die in the night, and then collects their cocks in the morning."**

**"Josephine, what're you talking about?" He leaped to his feet and stepped on his glasses. "Holy shit...I don't even know what bimbo means..."**

**But she flung herself on the bed inside and punched the wall as Kopfelman trailed in helplessly and wondered about his inherent genius for fucking things up when they seemed to be going right for a change.**

**"Josephine, please...I give you permission to mug me again."**

**"Just leave me alone."**

**"I didn't mean to upset you this way."**

**"Oh, bullshit!" Josephine reared up at him. "Are you really so blind that you can't see I'm no good for you, that I'm not the woman you think I am?"**

**"But..."**

**"What?" She snapped. "You think you're in love and you don't even know the first thing about me. I never had an unselfish thought or feeling in my life, and I do all my father's dirty work," she railed at him. "You have nothing at all to do with this, it's me, goddamn it, can't you see? I'm nothing...Nothing!"**

**"How can you even say such a thing!" He shouted fiercely, straining a part of his lower left back as he stumbled toward her passionately and tried to shake some sense into her. "Okay," he**

**said, "so you're down right now, and you're all choked up with the stigma of being disreputable..."**

**"I feel like a goddamn pizza waitress," Josephine cried.**

**"All right," he admitted, "it's obvious that you feel you've been used, and there's nothing you can do about it right at this moment, or who the hell knows how long it'll take, but what about the rest of your life?" He challenged her. "You want to know what nothing feels like? Let me give you a shot in the head so you think that you're the Abruzzi Strangler!"**

**Josephine laughed through all her tears and let him prop an arm on the bed to get close to her.**

**"I knew that you couldn't kill anyone."**

**"Well, the fat man almost killed himself when he got a look at your father's book."**

**"It's too bad it had to work out that way, about Nunzio drowning and dragging you into all of this."**

**"I'm not complaining."**

**"Yes, I know, but the whole thing it out of control right now. It's one big mess."**

**"The funny part is—I'm supporting the whole Zangara family."**

**"At least you have more than six months to live."**

**Kopfelman nodded appreciatively.**

**"For a while there, I was starting to plot like Bette Davis in Dark Victory. Remember that movie?"**

**"Is that the one where she dies of a tumor?"**

**"And Humprey Bogart's the stable boy."**

**"I'm so relieved that you're someone else."**

**"That's the nicest thing that anyone ever said to me, and I don't remember what anyone said."**

**"Oh, God," she shoved at him playfully, "the things you come out with."**

**"It must be because I don't sleep at night from thinking of you."**

**"You don't dream of me?"**

**"You won't even make a guest appearance."**

**Josephine cuddled up to him and regarded him with a look of delight she had never ever felt before.**

**"You look so much better with your glasses on."**

**"You think so?"**

**"Yes, too bad you bent the frame out of shape."**

**"The man said they were collapsible."**

**"But not on the floor."**

**"Well, you had me all excited there."**

**"That's another reason for not going back to the fat's man place. I don't want you getting involved again. It's too dangerous."**

**"But they have no way of knowing the truth, and we really can do a number on them."**

**"It's over our heads," she insisted firmly, "and what happens when they find out you're dead?"**

**"It won't make the papers at least for another day or two. It's not that important. A tourist drowning."**

**"I don't know," she said. "You're playing with fire."**

**"For five hundred grand I'm willing to burn my fingers a little! It's dirty money that's up for grabs and I have no qualms about using it as a cleaning agent for both of us, maybe open up a place somewhere in Greenwich Village for unknown artists."**

**"Is this a proposal?"**

**"It's more than that."**

**"It sounds like a little midnight madness."**

**"Why not?" He beamed. "You only live once."**

**"You've lived twice already."**

**"So already you're getting more for your money," he mimicked for her in a heavily accented Yiddish inflection. "Oh, yes, I forgot to tell you my name, it's the only thing I remember so far, except for the fact that I may be Jewish."**

**"What makes you think you're Jewish?" She asked.**

**"Every now and then, a familiar voice calls out to me: Marvin, you schmuck, come home already."**

***"Oy Vay!"* She laughed. "And you had to pick on *Nunzio Zangara*?"**

**"I picked up a room key. How did I know what was going on?"**

**"That's all you remember?"**

**"I remember being circumcised by Rabbi Schwartz, and my grandfather's name was Schlomo 'The Shlepper' Kopfelman."**

**"Are you kidding me?"**

**"That's the funny part, I don't even know."**

**"This is really getting hysterical."**

**"Are we having fun?"**

**"I'm delighted beyond my wildest dreams, but Carmine is all set to rub you out."**

**"So, we'll give him a little part of the business—the lobby concession."**

**He told her about his brief recollection before being mugged, and that somehow, somewhere along the line, he had something to do with a teacher's convention.**

**"That's why I'm possibly so knowledgeable when it comes to art."**

**"Then why take a chance of getting messed up with Al Gavona?" She swung back into command again. "This is not any game for amateurs. You're out of your depth."**

**"Well, I don't seem to have much choice in the matter. A man named Rinzi is coming to pick me up tomorrow, and where do I go between now and then for a quick escape when I don't have a passport—or even any past to go back to…unless someone comes to claim me here in the hotel lobby."**

**"Why the lobby?"**

**"Where else am I going to sleep tonight when I don't have a room?"**

**The implications were wide and clear.**

**"You can't stay here."**

**"Why not?" He asked. "Your brother?"**

**"No, we have separate suites."**

**"Then what's the problem?"**

**Josephine felt a sharp little tug where her heart used to be.**

**"You're making things very difficult for me."**

**"What's so difficult? Pull out the couch. I'll even sleep on the terrace if you want."**

**"It just doesn't seem the right thing to do."**

**"What's the right thing to do?"**

**"I told you before...we hardly even know each other."**

**"So give me a rope and I'll hang out the window all night long, but nothing too tight around the neck. Nothing intimate."**

**"You're impossible."**

**"Yes, but I'm on your side, and I want you to help me. I want you to do even more than that, but it's up to you."**

**The telephone rang.**

**"Carmine? Yes, I'm all right, sure...the whole thing was a big mistake. You were right all along. The guy didn't know which end was up. I got rid of him. No..."**

**She cupped the receiver and whispered fiercely to Kopfelman, "Already you have me lying for you?"**

**"Already you're talking with a Jewish inflection."**

**Josephine crossed and uncrossed her legs and positioned herself in such a way that in shifting about to be comfortable, her skirt had inched up dangerously above her thigh and threatened to spread like a centerfold.**

"No...No...No...The deal is off. It just doesn't make any sense anymore. I'll call New York. I'll see you tomorrow."

She clicked off the phone with a nervous grin and unselfconsciously tugged down at the hem of her dress as Kopfelman did his humble best not to fall at her feet and bury his face there in total subjection.

"What's the matter? You're all sweated up."

"It's warm in here." He opened his shirt and fanned himself. "I like the way you handled your brother."

Josephine lit up a cigarette and ducked it out. "The Chinese say if you save a life, it belongs to you."

"Is that what you're doing, you're saving me?"

"You know very well what I'm doing," she said. "I feel obligated. I somehow feel this is all my fault."

"So if anything happens, we'll take out a little no-fault insurance."

Josephine lowered her head on the pillow and pinched her nose, "All kidding aside, this whole thing is starting to get to me. I feel so depressed, I don't know what to do with myself."

"If you want to lie down, I'll go inside."

"No, stay," she said. "Don't leave me alone."

"Just a moment ago, you were laughing at me and having fun."

"I don't know how to explain it myself, but...I feel like I'm having labor pains..."

**"That's not so unusual." Kopfelman carefully positioned himself on the bed next to her and found out he was a whole head shorter. "Something is starting to stir in you and come to life that you probably never felt before."**

**"That's silly…"**

**"No, that's love, "he said. "It's either like short-term pregnancy or indigestion."**

**"Where did you ever hear such a thing?"**

**"It's common knowledge."**

**"Common to whom?" She turned on him. "Is that something that you read in Freud?"**

**"No, something that came up on me while eating your father's calamari."**

**Josephine flung the pillow at him.**

**"You sonofabitch!"**

**"I was only trying to make you laugh."**

**She playfully pinned his arms to the bed. "If I ever fell in love with you, my father would kill the both of us."**

**"Not if he knew about labor pains."**

**"You're not my type. You're too weak for me."**

**"At least you won't have to fight me off."**

**"You're the biggest mistake I ever made."**

**"I love you too," he winced at her.**

**And straddling him with body thrusts that ran from her pelvis through every tremor of Kopfelman's wildest fantasies, she bit at**

**his neck, then bit off a piece of his undershirt, and mysteriously all the lights went out.**

ထထ

# 10

**At first he thought he'd been mugged again, or that somewhere in the violent throes of unconsciousness, he had somehow managed to dislodge his spine and clear out all his sinuses, but gradually, as he came to himself, and felt the bruise of his dumb open mouth and discarded body, he realized he had skulled himself on the headboard of the bed while trying to switch positions with her in the steamy, inexplicable wilds of making love.**

**"Are you sure your brother will not unexpectedly barge in here and blow my balls off, in order to save the honor of the family?"**

**"The last thing Carmine would ever dream of is you and I making love together. He thinks you're a little spineless worm."**

**"You don't have to sound so cheery about it."**

**"Relax," she said. "You're the only man I ever made love to who managed to break the headboard of the bed before entering me."**

**"I'm sorry," he said. "I..."**

**"Nunzio, please..."**

***"My name is Marvin!"***

**"Marvin," she corrected herself, "a woman is always flattered by passion. You don't have to apologize."**

**Which sounded like someone telling him that in time he would learn to walk again.**

**"Were there many other men?" He sulked.**

**"I really don't want to go into that, but I will tell you this," she smiled at him, "you're the first man who ever satisfied me."**

**"Really?"**

**"Yes."**

**"I find that rather hard to believe."**

**"I would never lie about something like that."**

**"I didn't say you were lying, did I?"**

**"What're you saying? Come over here."**

**"I'm here," he said.**

**She reached out an arm to draw him near, but Kopfelman sulked even further away.**

**"Could it be that we're having an argument, and I don't even know the reason why?"**

**He didn't know what he was doing either, he realized, but something about the way she was talking was bugging the living shit out of him. Was he jealous because she had lived before, and loved before, and had a Past that he could not control—or was it something about himself that could turn a compliment upside**

**down and then get depressed when he couldn't find out what was wrong with it?**

**"So what's the problem?"**

**"Nothing," he said. "I must be getting your labor pains."**

**She strummed through his hair and was stringing it over a burgeoning bald spot that Kopfelman now grew conscious of.**

**"Do you love me?"**

**"No, I'm only here for the hunting season."**

**"Fuck you!" She said. "I'm serious."**

**"Yes, of course I love you! Kopfelman blustered. "Who else would wreck a bed for you while making love and then get angry at all the bedsprings!"**

**Josephine failed to get the connection.**

**"I don't even know what you're talking about. There are times I don't understand you at all."**

**"There are times I don't understand myself, so don't even let it bother you." He buried himself underneath the covers and wondered how a burgeoning bald spot could get on his head without his even knowing about it. "So Carmine thinks I'm a spineless worm?"**

**"I knew I shouldn't have told you about it."**

**"That's all right," he said. "I'm sure your family will welcome me with open guns."**

**"And what about your family?" She asked. "You haven't said two words about them."**

**"What can I say when I don't remember?"**

"Well, that's the thing that's been bothering me." She reached out and drew an arm around him and coaxed him to light up her cigarette. "What about all this amnesia bullshit? What happens when your memory returns and you finally get to know who you are?"

"I don't foresee any problems there."

"But suppose when you remember who you are, you forget who you were when you had the amnesia?"

"That's not impossible."

"No, it's not," she insisted. "I saw it in one of those old-time movies with Ronald Coleman and Greer Garson. They fell in love and then he gets hit by a taxicab and doesn't remember he's married to her and falls in love with another woman."

"I'd have to get hit by a guided missile to ever pull a stunt like that where you're concerned, you're the most important thing in my life."

"But how do you know there was nobody else before you met me, or—listen, maybe you might be married!"

"I might also be a homosexual."

"Don't get so smart."

"I'm not so smart," he fired back, "but I'm starting my life all over again, and I don't want to know about any fachacta amnesia movies or what went on before we met, which is really what got me started before," he finally admitted. "I'm crazy about you, all right?" He said. "And I don't want to hear about this guy this, and this guy that, and...okay, I'm jealous when it comes to these

**things, but as far as I can remember right now, you're the only woman I've ever loved or intend to love."**

**Josephine nailed him down again and smothered him with open mouth kisses.**

**"See what happens when you don't behave?"**

**"Does it bother you that I'm shorter than you and also weaker?"**

**"It's how you use what you have that counts."**

**"No Vince Lombardi bullshit talk."**

**"You don't have muscles, I don't have tits. You want to fucking argue about it?"**

**"Please don't curse."**

**"You sound like my father."**

**"Look, I want you to know that I saved your father a lot of money by filling in for this Strangler from Abruzzi schmuck. You don't pay a man for drowning on you in one of the world's great vacation spots."**

**"Stop acting Jewish."**

**"You want to know about Jewish, darling?" He zetzed her back. "The difference between a Jewish actuarial table and one put out by insurance companies in Italy is that Jews can predict the exact time and place of how and when you're going to die, but Italians will tell you where to find the bodies."**

**"You lousy rat..."**

**"Stop acting Italian."**

**They tumbled off the edge of the bed and onto the floor with Kopfelman begging for mercy.**

**"Okay," he said. "Forget the pizza. I'll have an order of whole wheat toast."**

**"I'll give you *orders*," Josephine struggled up with him. "What time do you have to be there tomorrow?"**

**"I have to be at the dock at three, then head on back to Big Al's place." He explained the preparations involved. "I leave for New York tomorrow night. As a matter of fact, they insisted that I leave today, but I told them I had a girlfriend here."**

**"That wasn't too smart."**

**"I said that I loved you, I never said I was very smart."**

**She threw on a robe and walked to the terrace.**

**"Why do I have this uneasy sensation that anything you do or say is one step removed from suicide?"**

**"Why, what makes you think I screwed up the works?"**

**"If anyone knows you have contacts here, if they even suspect..."**

**"They don't know anything. Stop getting carried away with yourself. I'll call you before I leave for New York."**

**"If you call anyone, they might get suspicious."**

**"Suspicious of what?"**

**"You better be careful!"**

**Kopfelman threw on a pair of pants and joined her on the terrace outside.**

**"Did you ever hear of Willie Wallenda and the Flying Wallendas? They used to be a high wire act."**

**"I've heard of them."**

**"Well, Willie once said that walking the tightrope was living…" Kopfelman underscored. "All the rest was waiting."**

**"Too bad he died while he wasn't waiting."**

**"He died?"**

**"He slipped!"**

**"I didn't know that."**

**"Well, neither did he, apparently."**

**"All right," he said.**

**"Make one false move…"**

**"I won't even move," he promised her.**

**A gust of wind blew in from the ocean with something of a spray in the air.**

**"It's so peaceful out here, I can almost taste it," Josephine sighed. "We run all around with our heads in the ground, and look what's out there waiting for us. I always wanted to live by the ocean."**

**Kopfelman studied the cosmic debris of the Pleiades, the Seven Sisters, and immediately thought of Tennessee Williams and Son of Sam.**

**"It's another world."**

**"I wish we were on vacation here."**

**"There'll be time," he said. "In New York we'll have our own vacation."**

**Josephine nodded absently, then reached into the cool night air as though she were trying to summon something from far away and beyond the grasp of both of them.**

**"It all seems so unreal to me..."**

**"It's real, all right."**

**"That's not what I mean."**

**She searched through the ever-elusive darkness for something more uplifting to say, something sound and true and also befitting the boundless depth of emotion she felt.**

**"If only...there was a moon out tonight."**

**She turned to him in utter frustration, an unlit cigarette in her mouth, and Kopfelman panned to the Pleiades.**

**"Who needs the moon when we have the stars?"**

**"Are you kidding me?"**

**"Why?"**

**"That's exactly what he says to her in *Random Harvest.*"**

**"Who says what?"**

**"Ronald Coleman," she cried.**

**"Will you please forget about Ronald Coleman and that stupid movie?"**

**Josephine bit off an angry flare from her cigarette lighter.**

**"I hope this is not a one-night stand."**

**"Oh, come on, now."**

**"I mean it," she said, "if anyone ever mugs you again..."**

**"If anyone ever mugs me again, I'm sure it'll be your brother Carmine."**

**"Carmine is the least of our worries."**

**"So who is it that we're worried about?"**

**"You're running against the entire clan."**

**"Your father?"**

**"Yes, he's old world religious."**

**"But occasional killings are okay too?"**

**"That's something that's not discussed in the family."**

**"Especially before the antipasto."**

**"No innocent victims, that sort of thing."**

**"The American way!"**

**"Are you frightened?"**

**"No, you're the best thing that ever happened to me, so how could we ever go wrong together?"**

**Josephine shivered and huddled herself inside the robe.**

**"I'm so fucking happy, I feel like a dope."**

**"You don't know how long I've been waiting to hear you say those words."**

**They clung together and Josephine started to cry again.**

**"What happens if you don't come back?"**

**"If I don't come back..." he broke a smile and tilted her chin toward a sudden onrush of light from the terrace directly above them, "just remember, kid, we'll always have Paris."**

ထထ

## 11

**At three o'clock the next afternoon, he talked her into seeing him off at the street pier where the boat was docked. He wanted them to see who she was. He didn't want them getting suspicious (as Josephine felt so sure they would) about how he had been spending his time, or with whom he had been spending it.**

**Rinzi, the driver, saluted him as he came on board.**

**"That's a nice piece of ass you got down there. No wonder you wanted your passport papers."**

**"You can't get laid without passport papers." Kopfelman flashed him a bogus smile of acknowledgement, but would gladly have rammed his entire arm down Rinzi's throat for having opened his vulgar mouth about Josephine. "So what's going on? Are we set for tonight?"**

**"Well, we had a little change of plans." Rinzi continued staring down at Josephine. "You're leaving on the midnight flight from the airport in Rio. We couldn't get clearance for Big**

Al's plane, so we'll shuttle you down there by helicopter, I'll do the driving. You better say goodbye to your friend."

Kopfelman gave a last-minute wave to Josephine as Rinzi revved the engine of the boat and made preparations for taking off.

"That's some hunk of woman," Rinzi grunted. "American?"

"Yes, I met her at the hotel bar."

"Her face looks kind of familiar to me."

"I thought you were only looking at her ass."

Rinzi got a kick out of that.

"It's too bad you're dying. We could've used a guy like you to liven things up."

"They seem lively enough without my help."

"No, the boss is very moody these days. His heart's on the bum and he eats like a fucking horse all day, which he ain't supposed to be doing, you know, and then he takes it out on us when he gets depressed—and last month he had a heart attack when he heard that the hit on Don Vincenzo didn't work out."

"Is there really that much money involved in losing your New York drug connection?"

"The moment the fucking Chinks took over we started losing a million a day."

"So the money I'm getting's a drop in the bucket."

"It's scratch-your-ass-money," Rinzi smiled. "But don't tell the boss I told you that."

The engine died.

**"What's wrong with the motor?"**

**"Sometimes it takes a while to get going. I think it's the fuel like."**

**Kopfelman turned toward the dockside gate and Josephine waved.**

**"I'm taking my girlfriend."**

**"Taking her where?"**

**"I'm taking her with me."**

**"The boss ain't gonna like that, pal, he warned you…"**

**"Nobody warns me, Rinzi!" Kopfelman flexed his hands together, then clenched them apart. "You ought to know my reputation. You really think I give a shit?"**

**"Hey, be my guest. The more, the merrier."**

**Kopfelman slipped down the sideboard railing, scrambled up to his feet again, then leaped onto the edge of the pier where the startled Josephine ducked instinctively, having assumed he was being shot at.**

**"What's going on?"**

**"I'm taking you with me."**

**"What're you crazy? I wasn't invited. Who said I could come?"**

**"I'm saying it, I'm inviting you," he beat his chest. "I'm the one who's sticking his neck out for them and doing all their dirty work, so what can they say if I take you along to spend a last few moments together? 'Don't do the job and kill Don Vincenzo—we're punishing you'?"**

"And when did you get this brilliant idea?"

"It's been kicking around my brain all night, and it just hit me like a ton of bricks that I can't leave you here...I can't go without you."

Josephine spotted Rinzi staring down at them.

"There's somebody up there looking at us like we're out of our minds."

"That's Rinzi, the driver. Don't worry about him, he's not too smart."

"Why, you think this is smart what you're doing here?"

"You don't have to go, I'm not forcing you."

"Then why is it that I can't move my arms?"

"I'm sorry," he said. He was holding her like a man possessed. "It's up to you."

"It's up to *me*?" She pretended she was adjusting his tie for the sake of the man who was watching them. "I've been telling you all along not to come here. I said it was wrong. I said don't go, forget it, you're out of your depth—and now you're making it my decision?" Josephine choked in the knot of his tie. "In Sicilian we have a word for you, it's *Cabro Thorsto*!"

"You're looking at this from the wrong perspective."

"I'll give you perspective," Josephine rattled away at him. "In your other Ronald Coleman life, you must have been a used car salesman.

"Listen," he said. "Would I ask you to come if I thought there was any danger involved?"

**"It's pushing our luck."**

**"But nobody's pushing," Kopfelman leveled out for her. "As far as they know, you're just a woman I met last night, which means absolutely nothing to them."**

**She heard her father's warning voice calling out to her like a prophet of doom: *He wouldn't know danger if it blew his ass off!***

**"What's wrong?" He asked.**

**"I'm beginning to think there's something wrong with the both of us. Come on," she said, "before I start having my head examined."**

**Kopfelman guided her gingerly up the side ladder to the deck above, and the moment they boarded, Josephine greeted everyone there in dumb bunny fashion, fixing her hair, making vain attempts at primping herself and apologizing for the way she looked, the dress she was wearing.**

**"Hey, Nunzio, where are you taking me?" She scanned the horizon as Rinzi set the boat in motion. "All I see are islands out there."**

**"Ask Rinzi, he's in charge of things."**

**"Are you the captain?"**

**"That's right," Rinzi beamed at her. "Do you know what line of work we're in?"**

**"Not really, why?"**

**"The place we're going is heavily guarded, so don't get scared. My boss is a very important man."**

**"I hope that I'm not intruding," she said. "I understand that I'm not exactly an invited guest."**

**"Don't worry about it," Rinzi leered and opened the throttle. "I forgot the boss was having a party for the Mardi Gras. There's gonna be plenty of people around.**

**"Any other uninvited guests?"**

**"No, just the Spics and local politicians out here who think they're all celebrities."**

**"With my kind of luck, it'll probably be a dress-up affair."**

**"Well, some people like to get undressed, if you know what I mean." He waited to get a rise out of her, but Josephine didn't bat an eye. "I'm not saying this applies to you, I'm just saying what goes on out there when people start drinking Coca Cola," Rinzi winked at Kopfelman. "We're coming in, do you see it out there?"**

**The island hovered off in the distance surrounded by mountains that loomed at them iridescently in the setting sun.**

**"That's breathtaking," Josephine pressed the rail. "Does anyone know the name of those mountains?"**

**"I know the name, but I can't pronounce it," Rinzi answered, straining until his forehead folded to meet his nose. "The one in Corcovado's the best. It's got a statue of Jesus Christ at the top of it."**

**"Did you know he was Jewish" Kopfelman quipped.**

**"Go fuck yourself! Excuse me." Rinzi apologized to Josephine.**

**"That's all right," she said. "He was only joking."**

**"Oh, Nunzio's got a wild sense of humor," Rinzi admitted, "but you don't fuck around when it comes to religion—like a few years ago, they put a car on top of that mountain to make a commercial. I think it was a Chrysler or something."**

**"Like Chrysler and Christ?"**

**"That's right," he said. "I mean, what the hell kind of bullshit is that? The water's polluted, you can't even breathe the air anymore, and they're even killing baby seals to get off their skin. Did you see that program on television?"**

**"No, I missed it."**

**"Yeah, when they show you all this blood on the snow of the baby seals and the whole thing is disgusting, you know? There oughta be a law against it."**

**Kopfelman agreed with him wholeheartedly.**

**"Never kill no one when it's snowing, Rinzi."**

**"It makes me sick just to think about it," Josephine yelped. "Defenseless animals...bashing their heads in...I wonder why people do such things?"**

**"Because some people don't have a taste for beauty!" Rinzi spewed out venomously. "They're so screwed up by their own inferiority complex, they take out all their revenge on creatures that can't fight back and defend themselves."**

**"How true that is."**

**"Well, some people don't wanna know the truth, which is one of the reasons our whole fucking country is falling apart and everyone's getting AIDS today."**

**"Is that the reason?"**

**"Sure," he said. "It's just another form of pollution."**

**"And where did you discover all this?"**

**"In the Reader's Digest."**

**Josephine made the fatal mistake of glancing over at Kopfelman, and both of them turned away from each other to keep from biting a hole through their cheeks as Rinzi ranted and raved at them for another five minutes, his gnarled, leather face and shopworn features sprawling with anger and unadorned hatred.**

**"You shouldn't've got me started on this," he apologized. "You guys wanna see the rest of the boat, just be my guest. There's plenty of liquor in the cabin downstairs."**

**Which is where they hurried for sanctuary.**

**"My jaw is aching," Josephine screamed. "I don't know how I kept a straight face."**

**"I bet he doesn't have one traffic violation to his name."**

**"And he doesn't litter."**

**"And he gives to all the charities."**

**"And he'd tear out your heart in sixteen seconds to make a score."**

**"And he's only the *driver*!" Kopfelman burst out laughing with her.**

**"I got news for you." She checked to see if her mouth was bleeding. "Everyone has their own rationale for not being evil."**

**"Is this how they manage to live with themselves?'**

**"Hey, nobody's bad when the whole world's bad."**

**"Is that the secret?"**

**"No," she said. "That's the bullshit that I've heard all my life, and I'm dropping out. I was dropping out before I even got out here." She discussed her buying a condo in the city and starting a whole new life for herself. "I've been working up the courage to tell my father about it."**

**"Your father will disinherit you anyway," Kopfelman was about to say, "as soon as he sees me," but then a depressing thought set in and rattled around all the edges of what she was saying to him, like somebody shooting dice in his brain.**

**"Speaking of dropping out," he said, "If big Al decides not to go ahead with the contract on your father, I'm shit out of luck."**

**"What do you mean, you're shit out of luck?"**

**"The only reason they're letting me go is to kill your father, otherwise I'm a prisoner here."**

**"And you waited till now to tell me about it?"**

**"I forgot all about it."**

**"You want to end up with the baby seals? Keep forgetting things."**

**"I'm beginning to have second thoughts about it."**

**"Oh, no, you don't," she cornered him. "The first thing you learn about making mistakes is you don't unmake them. The second thing is you can't afford to have second thoughts."**

**She could well understand his being screwed up from having amnesia and not knowing where he came from and stuff, but how could he blithely forget about things that were so important and then try to shrug it off on her in that well-meaning, lovable, fucked-up way of not even knowing which end was up, or what it was that was coming down?**

**"What I need right now is a good, stiff dose of Scotch in me."**

**"Are you angry?"**

**"No, I'm thrilled to death." She reluctantly threw an arm around him forgivingly, but felt like pouring a drink down his neck. "If Big Al wants to get rid of my father, he's certainly not going to back out now, so you're shit-in-luck, despite yourself."**

**"I should never have asked you to come along and expose you this way."**

**"You didn't exactly twist my arm, so stop feeling guilty." Josephine poured out a glass of Scotch and handed him one. "If there's one thing I can do very well, it's take care of myself—and fend for myself."**

**"And *fend* for yourself?"**

**"Why, you never heard that word before?"**

**"I remember the first time I ran across it in the Anglo-Saxon Chronicles."**

**"I'm glad you remember something," she said, "and don't be so cute. I know just as many as you do, bubby."**

**"And now you know *bubby*?'**

**"Just drink your drink before you get seasick."**

**"Kopfelman swallowed and coughed it up.**

**"This stuff must be here from Prohibition."**

**"We don't have ice cubes."**

**"Maybe I better not have any more, I might get drunk."**

**"It doesn't make any difference," she said.**

**"I don't want to make any stupid mistakes or screw things up."**

**"Then learn how to keep your big mouth shut before grass starts growing over it." She clamped his mouth before he could get in another word or come back at her. "Just remember, darling, to dig your own grave, you don't need a shovel."**

**"Is that one of your sage Italian proverbs?"**

**"Oh, no," she said. "It's the epitaph on my uncle's tombstone—Louie 'The Loose Lip' Matarazza."**

ᏅᏅ

# 12

The party was being held outdoors on Big Al's elaborate patio, with a rigged-up stage for the orchestra and dramatically string-lit trees and shrubbery down by the pool.

"No one is naked," Josephine cracked. "I feel like something the wind blew in."

"If you came in with a mop and pail and your grandmother's housedress, you'd still be the best looking woman here."

"You certainly know how to shoot the shit, I'll say that for you." But Kopfelman brought a glow to her face. "You really think I look all right?"

"You look absolutely smashing, dear."

The women were dressed in exotic gowns (to Josephine's casual pants-suit outfit), and all the men looked like Caesar Romero in white dinner jackets and white gleaming teeth—and "orgy" written in every line of their suntanned, heroic, smarmy features.

**"Listen, you better stay close to me. I don't trust these people," Kopfelman cautioned warily.**

**"All that we need here is Don Ameche and Alice Faye."**

**"Who's Alice Faye?"**

**"A very good friend of Carmen Miranda."**

**Kopfelman spotted Big Al Gavona looking his way.**

**"I better check in on with the fat man first. Just mingle, but don't get overly friendly."**

**"I'll mosey around."**

**"As a matter of fact, I think you should talk to that bald-headed guy."**

**"What bald-headed guy?"**

**"The one with the limp. He looks important."**

**"He looks like shit."**

**"Just behave yourself and don't get lost. I'll be right back."**

**The fat man greeted Kopfelman warmly, slopping around with a plate in his hand and tomato sauce on his upper lip.**

**"Did you eat yet?"**

**"No, but I'm really impressed by the spread you have—I mean, all this food and all these people."**

**"Society people." Big Al sucked on a ring finger knuckle to get at an errant fleck of linguini. "The finest people in all Brazil. Almost all of them are on the take, but they look good in clothes, these lousy Spics."**

**He introduced Kopfelman all around, then gave him a little warning nod and tug of the wrist.**

**"Stay sober, you hear? I wanna show you my painting later."**

**"The stolen Picasso?"**

**"Don't talk so loud."**

**"I assume you have the money also."**

**"I got the money. I also got a guy coming later who says he knows you. Stabile from Chicago."**

**"Stabile from Chicago?" Kopfelman lost complete sensation in both his legs. "How does he know me?"**

**"He says you done a job for him."**

**"How wonderful, like old home week."**

**"He says you iced an old friend of mine named Benny the Mole."**

**"Look…business is business," Kopfelman bluffed.**

**"I'm not saying nothing. I said old friend, so who gives a fuck?" the fat man eased diplomatically. "But Tony Stabile is friends with me, and I told him about my deal with you for Don Vincenzo. I said to him that you're dying of cancer, so Don Vincenzo sent you here to whack me out, and now I'm doing the same to him."**

**"There's nothing like getting a guy who's dying and finding him work."**

**"You sonofabitch, you got some sense of humor." Big Al banged at Kopfelman's back. "I hope that when it comes my time, I can do the same."**

**A couple approached them and Big Al unloaded his overstuffed plate on Kopfelman.**

"The guy who heads the rackets in Rio. His wife's a cunt. I'll get back to you later. Enjoy the food."

Kopfelman ditched the unholy mixture of pasta and something yellow looking, and searched through the crowd for Josephine, who was down by the pool with a drink in her hand and two men hovering over her with cigarette lighters.

"Sorry, gentlemen." Kopfelman almost ignited his thumb on a book of matches. "The lady and I have business to discuss."

She thanked them for lighting her cigarette and smiled at Kopfelman's panicky look of having been booked on the Andrea Doria.

"What's the matter?" She said. "You look like a ghost."

"I told you to talk to the bald-headed guy."

"Did you catch what's going on by the pool? There are two defrocked nuns there dressed to kill, who are killing themselves to undress each other, though nobody else seems to notice them."

"So Rinzi was right."

"He's been waving to me from across the pool."

"I don't like the setup. I think we better get out of here and take a walk."

"Wherever you go, it's all the same." She allowed herself to be dragged away in Kopfelman's death-grip protective custody. "My father, for all his obvious hang-ups and disrepute, does not own yachts, does not have a private island retreat with degenerate parties, and all of us went to Catholic school."

"Is that where you learned to handle a gun?"

**"Not only a gun. I can kick balls, gouge out your eyes, and also drive a getaway car."**

**"You might have to drive a helicopter before this is over," Kopfelman cracked. "There's a guy out here who's supposed to know me."**

**"Jesus Christ!"**

**"He's supposed to be coming later, or something."**

**"He's not here now?"**

**"No, Big Al just sort of dropped it on me. The man's from Chicago. Tony Stabile."**

**"I know him from when he was friends with my father, that rat fink bastard."**

**"What else do you know that might help save a life or two?"**

**Josephine plunged her head in silence.**

**"Josephine, did you hear what I said?"**

**"I heard," she said. "I'm thinking that maybe his plane might crash before he gets here."**

**"That bad, huh?"**

**"There's an outside chance that Fatty is bluffing."**

**"Why would he bluff at this late stage?"**

**"Who knows?" She said. "He's a psychopath. He's had people killed for just blinking at him. It could be almost anything at all, or nothing at all."**

**"Or maybe it's just a coincidence."**

"When somebody's into the mob for money—and doesn't get killed for not paying off—that's *coincidence*! Not somebody traveling three thousand miles to get to a party."

"It doesn't look good."

"What was Nunzio doing with Tony Stabile?"

"I think he was hired to kill somebody named Benny the Mole."

Josephine drew a blank on that.

"Was there anything that you said or did that might have cast a doubt in his mind?"

"I did everything you told me to do."

"And no one seemed suspicious at all?"

"Well, nothing important..."

"Everything is important right now. The smallest detail."

Kopfelman scanned the poolside crowd and zeroed in on one of Big Al's bodyguards.

"You see that guy with the pushed-in nose and tape on his ear?"

"The one who's giving us fisheyes?"

"Yeah."

"What about him?" She asked.

"Well, he passed a remark that...he thought I looked like some movie actor who always plays the part of a weakling."

"And nothing about that upset you?'

"No, what's wrong about it?"

Josephine felt her horns sticking out and pulled them in.

**"They don't believe you."**

**"What do you mean, they don't believe me?"**

**"They don't think you look like a hit man, Marvin, plain and simple. That's what my brother was trying to tell me, and God only knows why I didn't listen."**

**"What did he tell you?"**

**"He said that you looked like Woody Allen."**

**Kopfelman grew annoyed at this.**

**"I thought I looked like Mother Teresa."**

**"The man from Chicago might fail to see the humor of that."**

**"Well, so do I."**

**"Well, you don't have to get so touchy about it. There is a slight resemblance, you know."**

**"So what do you want me to do about it, push in my nose and tape my ears?"**

**"Just cool it."**

**"Sure, I'll jump in the pool with those two dykes down there and plead insanity."**

**"Please sit down."**

**"I can't sit down."**

**She nudged him into a seat next to her.**

**"That could be one of the reasons he's bluffing."**

**"I don't know what you're talking about."**

**"Then stop with the sweating and listen to me." She gracefully lowered a seductive smile at one of the passing bodyguards. "Big Al doesn't know what you look like."**

**"How do you know?"**

**"Because Nunzio rarely made contact with people. Whoever wanted to hire him out had to go through my father's organization. In fact, I never met him myself, which is why I didn't know who you were the first time I saw you, and neither does Fatty or anyone else because Nunzio only dealt through my father—except when he did his freelance jobs."**

**"Was Benny the Mole a freelance job?"**

**"I don't remember."**

**"Well, try to remember."**

**"I *can't* remember."**

**"Just clear your mind and concentrate."**

**"On what?" She snapped. "You think I keep a scorecard on this?"**

**"Joz-a-feena...pleeza...don't be that way."**

**"I told you before that I wanted out of this goddamn shit, and now I'm getting my face rubbed in."**

**"I thought you were going to fend for me?"**

**"I am," she said, "but only on weekdays."**

**Kopfelman felt a twinge of resentment thrusting against some rickety need to preserve himself.**

**"So you really think I don't look the part of a Nunzio."**

**"I wasn't trying to put you down."**

**"I know," he said, "but I don't like the odds."**

**Josephine drew in a long deep breath of star-spangled night with all the weight of heaven descending.**

**"I'm sorry, Marvin, I'm losing it all. This whole place is starting to give me the creeps."**

**"Then let's pretend we're somewhere else."**

**Such as where?" She groaned.**

**"A cross-country bus trip."**

**"What kind of trip?" She sat up straight and made a face. "I can think of other places to be."**

**"Of course you can. That's the point," he said. "It's the most unromantic thing I can think of to test if you really love someone—being trapped together and all scrunched up for days on end, with no escape, and tired as shit of looking at each other…"**

**"How the hell do you think of these things?"**

**"I look for the worst that could be the best."**

**"You mean there's more?" She burst out laughing. "I still have to take a bus trip with you?"**

**"At least you're laughing."**

**"God only knows what I'm in for yet."**

**"I think we're in for some fireworks."**

**The servants were setting up rockets and flares at the other end of the patio.**

**"Have you ever been on a bus trip with a woman you love?"**

**"I have never been on a bicycle with a woman I love!"**

**She gripped his face in both her hands and framed it there in a fit of startled appreciation.**

**"You're the most unpredictably honest person I've ever met...and sometimes I think you're a little insane."**

**"We may never know."**

**"It's not that important."**

**"What about you?"**

**"My worst has never been my best, so get me a drink and let's pretend we're enjoying ourselves."**

**He clicked his heels and gave her a deadpan Nazi smile as mad glints of reflected light from the fireworks exploded off the lens of his glasses.**

**"Tell me, is it safe?" he said.**

**"*The Marathon Man*."**

**"That's all that's missing, a few good Nazis."**

**"Wait until you meet Tony Stabile."**

**"It's time to get drunk."**

**He came back with drinks that were towering.**

**"I would like to have the hair spray concession for Latin America."**

**"Big Al's got it made down here, the sonofabitch."**

**"To Lady Luck," he clinked her glass.**

**"What're we drinking?"**

**"I don't know," he said, "but there's smoke coming out of the ice cubes."**

**"Pina Colada."**

**"Sounds like one of the numbers they're playing."**

**"Know how to dance?"**

**"No, Jews don't dance, we just levitate."**

**"Will you stop with the bullshit?"**

**"Nunzio probably had two left feet, not to mention his brain, so why call any attention to myself?"**

**"Come over here." She pressed a thumb to Kopfelman's nose and flattened it out pugilistically. "I like you better the other way."**

**"My worst or best?"**

**"You're not going to let me alone with that?"**

**"I want equal time."**

**"There's nothing to say. I've already told you the worst of it. My life has just been one big blah!" She played with something behind her ear, then nervously flicked out a cigarette and waved it back and forth at him. "Of course, there was my prom..." she said. "Is that what you mean?"**

**"I didn't know they had any proms in Catholic school."**

**"Oh, yes," she said, "but I wasn't allowed to go to mine. I wasn't even allowed to wear lipstick."**

**"Your father?"**

**"Yes."**

**"I couldn't get a date for my prom."**

**"I was ugly as sin."**

**"I was voted the boy least likely to attack anyone."**

**"I broke out in rashes whenever anyone mentioned sex."**

**"No girl would even look at me."**

"Why, Marvin," Josephine clapped her hands, "you're *remembering*!"

"Is that what I'm doing?" Kopfelman felt his stomach sliding up and out and down again. "Oh, boy," he said. "It's amazing how it slipped out that way without my even knowing about it."

"You must be getting your memory back."

"I don't even know if I want it back."

"Then, forget it."

"No, I can't forget it." Kopfelman suddenly rose to his feet in the middle of nowhere, not knowing what he was doing there with his mouth hanging open, or what it was that was coming next. "I'm taking you to that high school prom, come hell or high water…even if it's the last thing to do," he vowed to her. "Is that stupid?"

"Yes, it's hysterical."

"Well, it's also retarded, but who gives a shit."

"I'm deeply touched."

"I'm dying of hunger."

"Let's get some food before they run out."

He helped ease her through the milling crowd and noticed that he was clenching and unclenching his fist with rising contempt at all the pug-ugly henchmen in sight who were staring at them, all the Caesar Romeros flashing their teeth.

"I have the feeling we're being watched."

"Then don't make any more stand-up speeches," Josephine cautioned. "Nunzio never went for that."

**"I keep forgetting."**

**"I warned you about forgetting."**

**"Yes, but it couldn't be helped. I was angry," he said. "I was angry for the both of us."**

**"Well, don't get carried away with yourself, or both of us might get carried away."**

**The buffet table was strewn with every conceivable dish and delicacy of Italian cuisine—and Josephine almost had a fit.**

**"What's the matter?" He said. "You don't like the food?"**

**"It's my father's food. I mean, all of it. He must have used the whole fucking cookbook, that *sporacione*!"**

**Kopfelman swallowed uneasily.**

**"What's that yellow stuff swimming around over there?"**

**"That's rapa," she said. "It's turnips in *Torquemada* sauce."**

**"Do they happen to have any eggrolls around?"**

**"No, try the eggplant parmigiana *a la Matarazza*."**

**"I can't," he said. "Whenever I eat Italian food, I feel like somebody's beating me up."**

**"Are you kidding?"**

**"No, I always get nauseous."**

**"I love the way you come out with these things."**

**"It's not my fault."**

**"We're going to have a wonderful marriage."**

**"I almost died from eating your father's *Scungilli Scampi* that Big Al fed me."**

**"So what do you eat when you're not getting killed?"**

"King Pao Chicken and Shrimp Lo Mein."

"Is that where we're going on prom night, darling, to Chinatown?"

"I never promised you a tomato garden."

"You're really a riot."

"I'll settle for pasta with cottage cheese."

"Look who's coming."

Big Al sauntered over to them and drew a bead on Josephine by searching the air to sketch out who she was to himself. The old Sicilian conjuring trick.

"You don't look familiar."

Kopfelman offered an introduction.

"Josephine, meet Mr. Big Al Gavona."

Big Al looked her up and down suspiciously.

"You certainly know how to pick them, kid."

"She came up with the crowd by the pool. She's been kind enough to talk to me."

"Oh, the Esperanzas?"

"That's right," Josephine brightened for him. "I'm slumming."

"Good, enjoy yourself. I just gotta borrow your friend for a moment."

Kopfelman gave a farewell nod by tapping his head to indicate "the bald-headed guy," then dutifully followed Big Al and the bodyguard (who was called Daw-Daw) in a slow procession across

**the lawn, the fat man's legs trailing two steps behind the rest of his body.**

**"Watch out for the Esperanzas," Big Al warned. "The fucks don't like Italian food."**

**As they entered the house, which was ominously dark and otherwordly in contrast to the party outside, Big Al motioned across the room to someone who was hidden in shadows.**

**"I want you to meet a friend of mine. Tony, meet the Abruzzi Strangler."**

**Tony Stabile emerged from the shadows, a short stocky man with a face that looked like overbaked pizza, an oversized hat that came down to his ears, and black evening clothes that were so out of date and shabby looking, you almost expected the shirtfront part to come popping out with a neon sign that read: *Eat at Joe's*.**

**"Long time no see," he grinned maliciously, swishing around a toothpick in his mouth, and locking onto Kopfelman's thumb in a bone-crushing handshake.**

**"You done a little favor for me some years ago."**

**"In Chicago?"**

**"Yeah."**

**"The Windy City," Kopfelman smiled evasively. "I once knew a man who danced with his wife there."**

**"Benny the Mole did some dancing too."**

**"Yeah, that's what Big Al was telling me."**

**"You don't remember?"**

**"I don't keep a scorecard on things like that."**

**"His neck was broken in thirteen places."**

**"I enjoy my work"**

**"His balls were missing."**

**"Benny the Mole didn't have any balls."**

**The man from Chicago gave Kopfelman one of his graveyard looks.**

**"You still got that tattoo on your ass?"**

**"Is that how we did business together?" Kopfelman turned to Big Al with a mocking edge. "I scored the hit, then dropped my pants to show you the tattoo on my ass?"**

**"It ain't so funny," Big Al leveled seriously. "He says you don't look familiar to him."**

**"If I looked familiar, I would have been dead a long time ago! You know the way I operate. I always worked through the Organization. Don Vincenzo was my contact man..." He foraged through all the information that Josephine had discussed with him and grew more indignant with each receptive lie he told. "You have any doubts about who I am, you tell me about it. You don't have someone come three thousand miles to give me a fucking autopsy report."**

**"Hey, all we're doing is reminiscing."**

**"Is that what we're doing?"**

**"Of course," he said. "Just to straighten out doing business together. I hope you don't think we was breaking your balls."**

**"I think anyone who has ever seen me is doing time with Benny the Mole."**

**"Now, Nunzio, don't get carried away."**

**"Is this the kind of respect I get for risking my life to do you a favor?"**

**"Don't jump to conclusions."**

**"You don't want to go ahead with the hit on Don Vincenzo, forget about it!"**

**"Come on, Nunzio, don't be that way."**

**"Oh, no," he said. "This is bullshit talk!" He paused before a full-length portrait of Mussolini. "No more nice guy."**

**The fat man slobbered all over him.**

**"We hadda play it safe with you. We couldn't afford to take no chances." Big Al turned his wrath on Stabile. "I told you he was the real McCoy!"**

**"I thought he was a much bigger man."**

**"He's dying of cancer."**

**"Jesus Christ!" The man from Chicago lowered his head respectfully and crossed himself. "Nunzio, what can I say to you? We all gotta go."**

**"I don't mind going," Kopfelman tossed out tragically, "but I'll never see my family again. The money I made is all for them—in Abruzzi there…"**

**Tony Stabile embraced him in a heartwarming bear hug. "You're s standup guy, but we hadda be sure of what we was doing, you know what I mean?"**

**"Hey, no hard feelings, eh, *goomba*?" Big Al joined the both of them and took them around. "Let's go inside, I got a little surprise for you."**

**"Another surprise?"**

**"No, this one you're really gonna like."**

**He led the way to an ornate office that looked like an order of onion rings impaled in wood.**

**"The money is in the overnight bag. I want you to count it and then we'll sock it away for you in the helicopter."**

**Kopfelman idly leafed through the money with fluttering heart.**

**"I won't insult you by counting it."**

**"You're okay, kid, I appreciate all you're doing for me, and to show my heart's in the proper place—so you don't get any wrong ideas—I'm gonna show you my masterpiece."**

**"The painting?"**

**"Yeah. Cost six million dollars!"**

**"Big Al shoved back a secret panel and fiddled around with the combination of a bank vault door the size of a truck.**

**"Wait'll you see this. You'll come in your pants."**

**They followed him into an airless crypt inside the vault, and there on the wall that was facing them, resplendently lighted and framed in gold—Picasso's long lost "Man with the Flute."**

**"Whatta you think of it?"**

**Kopfelman studied the painting in depth and was one breath away from an honest appraisal of awe-struck appreciation and**

**wonder, when something went "pop" inside his head like a ten gun salute of deliverance.**

**"It's incredible."**

**"Yeah, I thought you'd like it."**

**"The best reproduction I've ever seen."**

**"What *reproduction*? What the fuck are you talking about?"**

**"I'm talking about the painting you bought for six million dollars. It's not authentic."**

**"You're outta your mind."**

**"You asked my opinion."**

**"You don't know what you're talking about..."**

**The fat man's neck blew out on him like a pregnant frog disgorging itself in labored breathing. "How can you tell from where you're standing? Go take a closer look for yourself."**

**Kopfelman feigned a closer inspection by running his fingers learnedly over delicate brush strokes and other facets of surface texture.**

**"What do you think?" He turned to Stabile, who almost swallowed the ever-revolving toothpick in his mouth. "Do you think it's a real Picasso painting?"**

**"What the hell'ya asking him for?" Big Al roared. "He don't know Picasso from fucking Prosciutto!"**

**"I figure we get another opinion."**

**"We don't need opinions. The painting's a fucking masterpiece. I even got the papers to prove it.**

**"I thought you said the painting was stolen?"**

**"Of course it is."**

**"Then how could you have any kind of papers on a stolen painting?"**

**"Look, don't give me any bullshit talk. The guys who stole it gave it to me as a guarantee."**

**"No artist puts down a guarantee that…yeah, that's right, that's my stolen painting."**

**Big Al's face lost all its color.**

**"You're breaking my balls."**

**"I'm telling you what I see up there."**

**"You're no fucking expert. How do you know it's a reproduction?"**

**"Peel off a layer of paint from the canvas. Test it yourself. If there's any other paint underneath of a different color, you know it's a phony."**

**"Where the hell did you hear this shit?"**

**"In the Reader's Digest," Kopfelman passed off airily. "Everyone knows that."**

**Big Al mopped at his neck and chin and held onto Stabile for support.**

**"I'm not too big when it comes to reading."**

**"Art imposters always paint over other paintings."**

**"Whatta we do then?"**

**"Very simple." Kopfelman took out a dime from his pocket. "Scrape along the edge of the canvas and see what happens."**

**"I'll ruin the painting."**

**"You won't ruin the painting. A dime's worth of painting can be restored, but how much is a forgery worth?"**

**Big Al ripped the dime from his fingers and scraped away at the bottom of the canvas: White flaked off and dark green showed from underneath.**

**"Those no-good, lowlife...ugh!" he choked. "Cocksuckers" was the last thing he said before hitting the floor and bouncing around with his arms and legs dancing wildly about him in rhythm to the music outside, his mouth awry, his eyes rolled back inside his head like an overloaded slot machine that had gone berserk.**

**Tony Stabile was paralyzed. "Is he kidding?"**

**"No, don't be alarmed. It's happened before when he gets excited." Kopfelman went through the studious motions of CPR (which had always struck him as deeply absurd and pornographic) by seating himself on Big Al's chest and squeezing his tits. "Go get the guy they call 'Daw-Daw' and tell him to bring the heart medication. Rinzi's got it."**

**Moments later, Big Al's eyes fluttered open again as Kopfelman dug around for a pulse.**

**"...what...the hell...happened...?"**

**"You just passed out. We've got to get you to a hospital."**

**"...medical center...downtown Rio...I own the place..."**

**Rinzi came back with the medication, along with Stabile and two other men named Zorro and Midge. They watched as**

**Kopfelman cradled Big Al's head in his arms and tenderly fed him the pills and water.**

**"Al, you want to postpone the job on Don Vincenzo?"**

**"...never...no...that Zulu fuck...go ahead as planned..."**

**"Maybe we ought to wait till later."**

**"...do it...*now*..."**

**"Then tell your men. I don't want any misunderstandings."**

**Big Al gave the sign to them.**

**"...he's got the contract...whatever happens..."**

**Kopfelman motioned Rinzi aside.**

**"We better get him out of here fast. His pulse is bad."**

**"Get a stretcher!" Rinzi shouted to the other men.**

**"How do you get him out of here?"**

**"We got our own private ambulance and special equipment."**

**"You know how to use it?"**

**"They never taught us."**

**"Who never taught you?"**

**"The guys who sold us the fucking equipment."**

**"Well, whatever you do—don't give him too much oxygen."**

**"Yeah, he ain't breathing right."**

**"That's the reason that you have to be careful."**

**Rinzi signaled to lower their voices. "Don't talk too loud, he looks upset. We'll leave in back to avoid excitement and take off from the heliport."**

**"Let's not forget what the big man said," Kopfelman whispered tactfully. "I'm supposed to leave for New York tonight. The money is in overnight bag in Big Al's study."**

**"I know," he said. "Stabile's got the money. The airport in Rio is only a mile from the medical center. The boss even had it named for him: *Gavona Pavilion.* There shouldn't be any problems at all about making your flight."**

**"Well, in all this excitement…"**

**"Don't worry about it. We've been through this kind of shit before."**

**"I'm sure you have."**

**"You wanna say goodbye to your girlfriend?"**

**"That's exactly what I was going to ask. I want to make sure she gets home all right."**

**"Just make it fast. We ain't gonna sit here and wait for you."**

**Josephine left the dance floor with the bald-headed man, saw Kopfelman, and excused herself.**

**"What's going on? You've been gone for a year. Are you leaving?"**

**"No, the fat man is leaving. I gave the momser a heart attack."**

**"You what?" She cried. She was so overcome she could barely speak. "How on earth did you manage that?"**

**"I told him his stolen Picasso painting was really a fake."**

**"He bought a fake?"**

**"No, I lied to him. I told him it was a reproduction," Kopfelman glowed excitedly. "I said that if he scratched beneath the surface of the painting, he'd find another painting there—and the truth is that Picasso always painted over his other paintings."**

**"Why would he do a thing like that?"**

**"Because every genius hates to admit he made a mistake, so rather than throw a canvas away that he didn't like, he would paint another painting over it."**

**"Marvin, darling, if bullshit could kill, you'd be dangerous!"**

**"No time now for compliments. Have you got a way of getting back?"**

**"The bald-headed guy's got the hots for me. He has a yacht and probably owns half of Puerto Rico. Don't worry about it."**

**Kopfelman then explained the setup with getting Big Al to the hospital.**

**"I'll call you at your hotel tonight before taking off on the flight to New York. I have to run."**

**"Did you ever meet the man from Chicago?"**

**"Yes," he waved. "He danced with his wife but he never met the Abruzzi Strangler."**

ꝏꝏ

## 13

**Big Al's body accounted for almost all the space on the helicopter, wedged in barely inches below the roof of the cabin and teetering on a stretcher there with not enough room for breathing space. Tony Stabile and the other two men, Midge and Zorro, were seated in back with Big Al and the overnight bag, and Kopfelman sat up front with Rinzi, who also happened to be the pilot.**

**"How is Big Al doing back there?"**

**"He ain't so good. He says he has these terrible gas pains."**

**"Just pray that he doesn't cut one loose in here or we're all a goner," Kopfelman mumbled. "How long will it take to get there?"**

**"Ten more minutes."**

**"I didn't know you could fly a plane."**

**"I do everything here, but nobody seems to appreciate it," Rinzi whined. "The money is in the bag by Stabile, in case you think I forgot about it."**

**"It never crossed my mind."**

**"I never seen him this bad before."**

**"It could be another false alarm."**

**"I hope you're right, but...the whole thing just don't make sense to me. He was feeling so good and happy tonight, and then Tony told me he got all excited about something to do with a fucked-up painting."**

**"The stolen Picasso was really a fake."**

**"And that's what got him all screwed up, a thing like that?"**

**"What can I tell you?" Kopfelman waxed philosophical. "Remember what you told me before about some people don't have a taste for beauty?"**

**"What has that got to do with the boss?"**

**"Well, sometimes when you don't have the taste and try to steal it, that's what happens."**

**Rinzi's eyes crossed over slightly, deep in thought.**

**"I don't understand what you're talking about."**

**"I'm talking about pollution, Rinzi—people like Big Al who are ripping off what they can't possess and bleeding it dry—just to hang up the skin of those baby seals!"**

**"I don't wanna hear that kind of talk."**

**"I thought we had something special between us."**

**"Well, that's between us and nobody else." The roar of the chopper was deafening and Kopfelman's voice could barely be heard, but Rinzi wasn't taking chances. "Don't talk so loud. Those guys in the back are fucking morons. I don't want them**

**knowing what I think about things—and don't ever mention them seals again! It reminds me of my mother in Jersey who don't know what kind of work I do."**

**"I'm sorry to hear that."**

**"Yeah," he said. "I told her I work for IBM."**

**"That's very good work."**

**"Well, my mother likes those initial places."**

**Kopfelman gave a solemn nod of commiseration.**

**"Listen, Rinzi, I like your style, and as soon as all this confusion is over and settles down, I'm going to show my appreciation from deep in the heart of that overnight bag."**

**"That's all right," he said, "you don't have to do that."**

**"I want to do it," Kopfelman laid on a comforting hand, "because people like us have to stick together and help each other, and don't forget that beauty is in the eyes of the beholder."**

**"I like that line."**

**"There is more in heaven and earth, my friend, than there is in all your philosophies."**

**"Where did you hear that?"**

**"I got it from *Playboy*."**

**"I must've missed that fucking issue."**

**"I think we're going to be very good friends."**

**"I like you, Nunzi. Nobody ever talks to me here. They just like to give me orders, you know?"**

**"It's because they feel inferior to you," Kopfelman piled it on for him. "They're jealous of all the things you can do."**

**"I could'a gone to college, you know."**

**"You're the only one with brains around here."**

**"The only thing is they threw me outta fucking high school for falling down a staircase with my homeroom teacher."**

**"How much they pay you?"**

**"I don't even wanna talk about it," Rinzi soured.**

**Kopfelman lowered his voice a peg, and crossed his eyes the way Rinzi did when concentrating.**

**"Get me to the church on time, there's ten grand right off the top for you."**

**"That's a lot of scratch."**

**"I don't want to have any accidents."**

**"What accidents?"**

**"I don't like the looks of Tony Stabile."**

**"Well, he represents Chicago, you know, like we gotta give him a little respect."**

**"Is he the one who's taking over if Big Al dies?"**

**"Nobody knows who's taking over. Big Al never appointed nobody, the greedy fuck! The whole operation might fall apart with no one around to keep things in place. It's gonna be a madhouse here, like dog eat dog."**

**"You don't look too happy."**

**"I may be out of a fucking job."**

**"Have you got any special place I can reach you?"**

**"Down by the marina, why?"**

**"I may be able to help you out."**

**"You only got six more months to live."**

**"And how much longer does Big Al have?"**

**Rinzi squinted anxiously.**

**"Later," he said. "This is no time to talk. We're coming in for a landing now."**

**"All I see is a rooftop there."**

**"That's all we need. I been making this trip so many times, I feel like a fucking taxi driver."**

**"In other words, he might still pull through?"**

**"He's done it before, but each time it keeps getting worse for him."**

**As soon as they landed, the operation for having to unload five hundred pounds of Big Al's stretcher from the narrow ramp of the helicopter to waiting attendants down below was as complicated as pulling in towlines in order to land the Goodyear blimp, while Rinzi, in the midst of it all, was shouting directions to doctors and nurses as though he were speaking to anthropological retrogrades from some Amazonian rain forest.**

**"These fucks don't know one word of English," he cursed to himself. "Easy, take it easy there!"**

**The fat man's eyes rolled open at them and fluttered weakly the moment he was safely placed.**

**"Hold it!" Rinzi silenced them. "I think the boss wants to tell us something."**

**Everyone gathered about the stretcher and strained to listen.**

**"...ain't gonna die...till Don Vincenzo gets it...first..." He fixed his gaze on Kopfelman, then moved his head toward Tony Stabile. "...want Nunzi on that plane tonight...no time to waste...give him...the money..."**

**Tony Stabile delivered the money reluctantly.**

**"Don't worry, Al, you ain't gonna die. Everyone here is rooting for you."**

**The cheering section, Kopfelman thought. He could not believe the unlikeliness of the scene he was in as they all piled into the overloaded elevator, then solemnly followed the stretcher into the sacrosanct halls of Intensive Care, where everyone looked so completely spooked and out of place, they nervously sought to avoid each other and tiptoed around the waiting room as though they were making the stations of the cross.**

**Tony Stabile spoke up at last.**

**"Where did Rinzi go?"**

**"He hadda sign something for the doctors inside."**

**"I hope these doctors know what they're doing." Tony Stabile paced back and forth, then jabbed out a finger at Kopfelman. "If anything happens to the big man in there, you check with me. The word from Chicago is hands off Don Vincenzo. Period!"**

**Kopfelman did a double take.**

**"I don't understand."**

**"If Big Al dies, the hit is off. His word ain't worth a fucking shit if he ain't around to enforce it, right?"**

**"I thought you guys were in this together. I thought you were friends."**

**"I ain't got no friends. I just got connections. The mob don't want no part of it."**

**"Then why did you let him deal with me to make the hit?"**

**"Cause we ain't got no jurisdiction here. We hadda play the whole thing by ear. That's the orders I got."**

**"And who gives the orders?"**

**"That's none of your fucking business, kid."**

**The Mafia's answer to dialectics.**

**Kopfelman felt the weight of the bag growing lighter and lighter.**

**"In other words, if Big Al dies, I give back the money."**

**"No, we're gonna let you jerk off with it!"**

**"I'm not that stupid," Kopfelman countered. "I'm trying to figure where you come in."**

**"I don't come in. I don't give a shit for Don Vincenzo or Big Al, either. I only do what they tell me to do, so if Big Al lives…you do whatever you gotta do, and the rest I don't wanna know about."**

**"Right now I have to go to the bathroom."**

**"Don't get lost."**

**"Why, you think I'll disappear with the money?**

**"Oh, no," he smiled. "We got people all over the place downstairs. Security measures. No one gets in, and no one gets out. You want us to hold the bag for you?"**

**"No, that's all right. I'm starting to get attached to it."**

**The moment Kopfelman left the room, he raced for a phone booth—and froze as Rinzi passed him by.**

**"Whatta you doing?"**

**"I'm calling my friend to see if she got back all right."**

**"She's probably fucking her brains out right now."**

**"Well, we have to give her time to get home and clean up a little, go to the bathroom…"**

**Rinzi got a charge out of that.**

**"She's the type, you gotta bite off her toes and put her in place."**

**"I didn't know you liked her that much."**

**"Yeah, give me her number before you leave."**

**"You sonofagun, you…" Kopfelman winked obscenely at him in the wholesome spirit of smut and sex. "I think you might be too big for her."**

**"Hey, come on, now!" But Rinzi instinctively reached for his crotch. "Ain't nothing too big for a cunt like that."**

**Kopfelman made up a telephone number and gave it to him.**

**"Don't forget about the offer I made."**

**"I'm thinking about it. Don't worry about it. I just hope that the boss don't die."**

**"Any new developments?"**

**"Nobody tells you nothing around here. Bunch of gooks. I'm going for something in the coffee shop. You want anything?"**

**"Yeah, see if they have a Barbie doll for overnight flights."**

**Rinzi laughed uproariously, then lumbered his way to the coffee shop and browsed around for something to read with his cup of coffee, thinking of how he would fuck out the brains of that hot ass *putana* the Abruzzi Strangler was leaving behind, when something from one of the local newspapers caught his eyes: *Underworld Figure Victim of Drowning.* A front page photo passport picture, blotched and runny and unfamiliar, had Rinzi reading further down to the caption below: *Mafia hitman, Nunzio Zangara, "The Abruzzi Strangler," found dead on beach by local police. Story, Page five.***

**He read the story several times until it began to dawn on him that the man in the booth and the man in the picture were...not...the...same...man!...How the hell could that be, he thought? He crossed his eyes and creased his forehead. How could there be two Abruzzi Stranglers?**

ꝏꝏ

**Kopfelman dropped in three more coins.**

**"Yes, I'm calling you from the hospital here, the medical center, so listen—there's a lot of crazy stuff going on, but your father's problems are over, bubby. The heat is off." He explained the new situation to her as dictated by the man from Chicago, including the part about having to give back all the money.**

**"Forget the money. Just give it back and get out of there as soon as you can."**

**"I was starting to feel so nice and pregnant."**

**"Don't take chances. Don't give them any…"**

**Rinzi appeared outside the booth with a huge automatic pressing against the glass of the door, at the level of Kopfelman's Adam's apple.**

**"You better hang up and come outside."**

**"What happened? What's the matter with you?"**

***"Marvin, what the hell's going on?"***

**"Get outta there!" Rinzi ordered him.**

**Kopfelman let the receiver dangle.**

**"…Marvin, who's that talking to you…"**

**"I was trying to set it up for you with Josephine."**

**"Stop fucking around and drop the bag—and don't make any sudden moves."**

**"This is absolutely ridiculous."**

**"Just get your hands up."**

**Kopfelman dropped the bag by his feet and raised his hands as Rinzi frisked him thoroughly.**

**"Where's your passport?"**

**"At the hotel, why?"**

**"You're in very deep shit."**

**"Will you tell me, please, what's going on?"**

**Rinzi shoved the paper at him.**

**"Who are you?"**

**There it was, all right. The ugly truth he had carefully avoided. The photo of Nunzio glaring at him with its startling features of Cro-Magnon man in full-blown vengeance.**

**"Why don't you give me some breathing room?"**

**"Don't tell me what to fucking do, you little scumbag! Who the fuck are you?"**

**"The Avon Lady," Kopfelman sputtered. "What do you want me to tell you, Rinzi?"**

**"Who do you work for? Who sent you here?"**

**"You're not going to like this..."**

**"Just keep talking."**

**Kopfelman was about to unravel the unlikely mess of his whole life story when Josephine's voice cried out to him in almost inaudible filtered whine from the dangling receiver *"...the FBI...you stupid schmuck..."***

**"All right, Rinzi, the game is up, I'm Federal Agent *Rufus T. Firefly*...FBI, Narcotics Division. Anything that you say right now may be held against you in a court of law."**

**"You sonofabitch!"**

**"Put down the gun, you're under arrest. The woman you met is my undercover contact here."**

**"I should've known you was too fucking smart to come from Abruzzi."**

**"And you're too smart to take the rap for everyone else," Kopfelman brainstormed feverishly. "I'm talking about cooperation. Immunity from prosecution. The federal witness**

**protection program. You help us out and we'll give you a new identity…with a guaranteed income to match your own."**

**Rinzi lowered the gun a moment.**

**"Which is fifty grand."**

**"With a bonus, of course."**

**"What kind of bonus?"**

**"It all depends how fast you get me out of this place before anyone else sees that photograph." Kopfelman kicked at the overnight bag by Rinzi's feet. "There's plenty in there for everybody. All I do is change the amount of money involved when I make my report—and write it off to cooperation."**

**Rinzi stared suspiciously.**

**"Is that legal?"**

**"No, but I don't want to be a dead fucking hero with somebody putting my ass in the grave, and I'm willing to pay the price for it."**

**The logic of this ebbed visibly through Rinzi's mind like molten lava.**

**"How much are we talking about?"**

**"Whatever you can fit in your pockets."**

**Rinzi stashed the gun away, then took it out and gave it over to Kopfelman. "I don't wanna take up too much room." He emptied out the rest of his pockets and then went to work on the overnight bag.**

**"All right, enough! I've got to have some evidence left."**

**"I'm risking my fucking life for you."**

**"There's somebody coming."**

**Kopfelman fumbled the gun inside the waistband of his pants and Rinzi shoved back the overnight bag like somebody who had swallowed something that wouldn't go down.**

**"Hey, where the fuck have you guys been hiding?" Midge strode down the length of the corridor waving his hands. "The boss is dead. You both better come on back inside."**

**Rinzi straightened up at once and patted down the bulge of his pockets.**

**"Jesus, what a shame," he said. He dropped his jaw as a sign of mourning. "He ate himself into the fucking grave."**

**"And just last week he was on a diet," Midge lamented, "of only eating four times a day."**

**"Are we bringing back the boss's body?"**

**"Whatta you think, we're gonna fucking leave it here for the Weightwatcher's Club?"**

**"I was thinking about the chopper, Midge."**

**"What's wrong with the chopper?"**

**"One of the rooftop pilot lights isn't working right, and all the weight puts a fucking strain on the hydro system."**

**"There's nothing we can do about it. You better fix it right away. All we need is another fucking accident."**

**As Rinzi got in the elevator, Kopfelman made an abortive attempt to follow him.**

**"Hey, Nunzio, did you hear what I said? Stabile is waiting," Midge persisted. "Where you going?"**

**"Well…maybe Rinzi needs help up there."**

**"You need any help?"**

**"No, it's just a matter of making a little switch adjustment." Rinzi carefully folded the paper with Nunzio's picture and tossed it over at Kopfelman with a parting grin. "It shouldn't take long. I'll be right down."**

**By which he meant: Goodbye forever.**

**Kopfelman saw his whole life lit up with Menorah candles.**

**"What's the matter, Nunzi, you all upset 'cause the boss is dead?"**

**"Yes, I'm all upset."**

**"You coming?"**

**"Yes, but I have to make an important call. I won't take more than two or three minutes."**

**"They want you now."**

**"By the time they sign the death certificate, make the arrangements, release the body—what's the rush?"**

**"All right, go 'head, but don't take too long, 'cause Stabile wants the fucking money back."**

**Kopfelman picked up the dangling receiver. The line was dead. He pretended dialing and waited for Midge to disappear before making a dash for the elevator—now in use—and bounded up a stairwell of the fire exit for three whole flights with his tongue hanging out. When he reached the roof, it was too late already. Rinzi was circling overhead and signaling down with his thumb and forefinger, blowing kisses, shouting at him through**

**the deafening roar of the helicopter. "Gotta protect them baby seals."**

**"You stupid bastard, don't you know you're a fugitive now with stolen money?"**

**Rinzi answered by buzzing the plane over Kopfelman's head in a last huzza.**

**"See you in court, you four-eyed fuck!"**

**Kopfelman hit the deck of the roof and almost felt like staying there, his last hope gone of getting away with the money intact, and silently praying for some sort of instant epiphany to help see him through the mess he was in with Tony Stabile and his merrymakers, all of whom might be looking to play a tune on his head if, God forbid, they should take it in mind to count the money—or maybe set hands on a local paper with Nunzio's underachievement in swimming a sure-fire way of getting himself even further submerged, Sicilian style.**

**He got up and flew down the stairs again, racing halfway past the coffee shop and almost upending an orderly who was unloading bags of dirty linen and stuffing them into a vent in the wall.**

**"Sorry," he said, "I…"**

**Kopfelman came to a screeching halt and backtracked to the vent in the wall as though it were there by divine intervention, some Cosmic Eye in which all contradiction resolved itself—his epiphany!—his last-ditch effort at beating the odds, for if no way**

**of getting out remained with Rinzi gone, then let him be gone with all the money!**

**"Does all this go down to the laundry room?"**

**"No comprende, senor."**

**"No...habla Ingles?"**

**"No, habla, no."**

**But the bags were disappearing fast, and as soon as the orderly finished unloading and turned to leave, Kopfelman dumped the overnight bag down the laundry chute and staggered into the waiting room with the disheveled look of someone who had been mugged again, or forcibly raped by an extraterrestrial.**

**"Get him."**

**"He's falling."**

**"What the hell happened?"**

**"Get him some water."**

**"What's going on here?"**

**"Where the fuck is the bag with money?" Tony Stabile rattled Kopfelman's head up against the wall and shoved a glass of water at him. "What'd you do with the overnight bag?"**

**"Rinzi..." Kopfelman gulped at them, "...as soon as he heard that Big Al died, he must have had a fit or something."**

**"What the fuck are you talking about? I thought he was getting the helicopter fixed?"**

**"That's what I thought too, but then he came back and grabbed me out of the telephone booth and..." Kopfelman felt a pain in his chest from doubling over and realized it was Rinzi's**

**gun digging into him, and that any sudden move of his might dislodge the position of the gun or make it go off inside his pants in frightful contradiction to his story. "...that sonofabitch put a gun to my head and stole the bag."**

**"He got the bag?"**

**"With all the money."**

**"You shitting us?"**

**"No, that's probably why he faked the business with the pilot light bullshit." Kopfelman repositioned himself to relieve the pressure of Rinzi's gun and hide the bulge. "He must have had the whole thing planned in order to make his getaway."**

**"That crazy bastard!"**

**"That's what I told him. I tried to tell him how crazy it was for thinking he could screw you this way, but all he kept saying was..." Kopfelman seemed to think better of it and shook his head.**

**"What's the matter?"**

**"I better not say it."**

**"What was he saying?"**

**"It's very insulting."**

**"What was he saying!"**

**"He said you suck toothpicks the way you suck cock."**

**Stabile exploded.**

**"Get that no-good motherfucker."**

**Everyone flew out the door at once in a frenzy of colliding bodies, while Kopfelman waited...one...two...three...and stalked**

**his way to a stairwell at the opposite end of the corridor, which led him to a back exit ramp where a truck was being loaded with laundry and dirty linen.**

**"Where's the laundry room?"**

**"Al dientro," a worker pointed inside.**

**Kopfelman leaped up the side of the ramp and followed the men to a room inside where two other workers were marveling over a strange black bag they had obviously just discovered there.**

**"Allright, hand it over and no one gets hurt." Kopfelman pulled out Rinzi's gun and plunged forward from the weight of it. "Not the laundry bag—the *other* bag!"**

**He grabbed the bag and backed down the ramp to the laundry truck, and the driver leaped out immediately with his hands in the air.**

**"No me molesta!"**

**"Is this stick shift? Do you speak any English?"**

**"That is not so working a very good truck."**

**"Yeah, give my regards to Old Broadway."**

**He raced the motor and nothing moved. He tried again, and something seemed to be holding him back.**

**"Emergencia."**

**"What are you saying?"**

**The driver motioned down at the floor to indicate the emergency brake, then leaped for his life as the truck shot out and climbed the pavement, crashed its way down a narrow lane of neatly parked cars, swung straight again, and almost killed an**

**itinerant worker and two of Big Al's bodyguards who were stationed at the back entrance ramp of the hospital.**

**They picked themselves up and started firing.**

**"Come back here, you little prick...You're fucking dead!"**

**Kopfelman zoomed through two or three "No Entrada" signs, went skidding past a construction site (where he shattered apart the barriers of an unfinished, unpaved four-foot embankment) and roared off into outer space with the sudden, startling realization—before making contact with the street below—that somehow, somewhere along the way, he had never learned how to drive a car.**

ooo

# 14

When he came to himself, he crawled out through the passenger side of the opened truck and raced through the crowded thoroughfare of the *Rua Visconde de Caravalas*, the name which kept repeating itself like a mad refrain as he frantically searched behind for pursuers and sprinted blindly, dragged down by the gathering weight of the overnight bag until he couldn't breathe anymore and slowed to a walk, his glasses dripping and fogged with sweat.

If only he knew where the hell he was going, or what he was doing, or where he was? But then, again, if he didn't know, then they didn't know, and such was the state of mind he was in that—bordering on the threshold of delirium—Kopfelman saw in this crassly simplistic *mise en scene*, not only a foolproof design for living, but also a fount of Talmudic wisdom that flowed through every part of his being like Wonton soup.

It was there at the first major intersection that police began rerouting traffic for the throng-filled streets of the Mardi Gras,

**one of which had been cordoned off for an endless procession of marching bands and garish floats and costumed revelers dancing and chanting everywhere.**

**"Pardoname!"**

**A lame-looking woman with rouged-up features and shopping bag peered up at him with a look of amusement.**

**"You American?"**

**"Yes."**

**"I like your watch. You have something in the bag for me?"**

**"I have nothing in the bag for you." He turned to leave, and then it hit him that maybe she was a contact for him through Josephine. "Do you know me?"**

**"No."**

**"Who are you?" He asked.**

**"Why, who do I look like, Monica Lewinsky?"**

**"Did Josephine send you?"**

**"No," she smiled, "I send for myself." She limped toward him aggressively with one leg slightly shorter than the other. "I do fuck for you."**

**He was so exhausted and near collapse, he thought that perhaps he had not heard correctly.**

**"What did you say?"**

**"What's the matter?" She barked. "You no understand the English language? I suck your balls. I like to put my tongue up your ass."**

**"Oh, no, I'm sorry…you have the wrong person."**

**"You no like women. You only like men?"**

**"I only like to get out of here," he backed off diplomatically. "I wish you luck."**

**"I do cheap for you with string and ice cubes."**

**The montage effect.**

**"I have to be going."**

**"I give to you nice so you always remember that maybe you wanted to marry me."**

**He moved out quickly, doubling back to an outlying area not as crowded, when somebody screamed and a hospital van appeared out of nowhere and jumped the sidewalk.**

**"There's the fuck!"**

**He bolted down a vest-pocket alley and hurled a fence to a steep embankment that dropped off into another alley, running until his lungs gave out by a garbage-ridden, junk-piled lot in some godforsaken neighborhood that one never saw in the tourist posters of Old Brazil, but the sort of place they loved to show in TV commercials of terrified women whose cars had broken down on them in the middle of nowhere, stranded alone on a dark, rainy night and wondering who would get to them first, the tow truck or the menacing shadows lurking at them from everywhere, and that everyone knew were really the shvartzas waiting to shut them up good and plenty for not having serviced their broken-down cars with the right motor oil or proper die-hard battery.**

**A footstep sounded from far away—or was it a footstep?**

**Kopfelman ducked to his knees on the ground and strained at something rustling back and forth at him in the eerie silence and uneven contour of moving shadows across the way, behind an abandoned baby carriage.**

**What the hell was wrong with him? Was he cracking up? Was he starting to hear those voices again? He reached inside the overnight bag for Rinzi's gun, but no one was there: a lunar landscape, completely deserted and fraught with menace. Behind him was the wall of the alley. Directly below was a junk-piled lot. He certainly couldn't go back where he started even if he could find the way and retrace his steps, which he knew he would never be able to do under any conditions. He simply had no sense of direction. All he could do is rest here awhile and try to gather his wits about him until they had tired of looking for him.**

**He blinked his eyes and listened again to the sound of something he couldn't distinguish, fighting fatigue and the urge to sleep…for just a few moments…to rest his eyes until he could gather the strength to run…to recuperate…a second wind…**

**"He runs around like a chicken with his head cut off, and then he wonders why he's always lost," his father yelped. "He doesn't know what world he's in."**

**"I'm resting."**

**"All your life you've been resting, so what else is new?"**

**"I'm involved with a woman named Josephine."**

**"Who's Josephine?"**

**"The woman I love."**

**His father's voice was silent a moment.**

**"Josephine's not a kosher name."**

**"I don't want to argue. She's waiting for me at the Hotel del Rio."**

**"And you're waiting here for a second wind with maniacs chasing after you?"**

**"I don't know how to get there from here."**

**"You're a basket case!" His father gave explicit directions. "It's west of here, by the *Rua Tenente Possolo*."**

**"West of *where*, the baby carriage? How can you tell directions from here?"**

**"You see your hands? Take a look at your hands. You know your left from your right?"**

**"Of course."**

**"And you can't tell the difference between east and west?"**

**"I can tell the difference," Kopfelman chewed on a piece of chicken that tasted like warmed-over kindling wood. "But how can you tell when your left and right aren't north and south?"**

**"Well, you gotta know what direction you're facing."**

**"But how do you know that?" Kopfelman anguished. "What has that got to do with your hands?"**

**"I never heard such a *mishegas* of confusing questions in all my life." His father turned to Kopfelman's mother. "Have you finished poisoning all the food?"**

**"Will you leave him alone till he's finished eating?"**

**"Are you going to sing or give advice?"**

**"I don't want him falling in love with people, especially strangers we don't even know if they have a disease."**

**"That's none of your business."**

**And right on cue, his mother emerged from the kitchen inside and blasted away at the top of her lungs through the nozzle of the vacuum cleaner: *"There's no business...like show business..."* while Kopfelman's father retracted into a knowing wink and nod of the head.**

**"You see now what I'm talking about? It's in the genes. It runs in the family."**

**"I thought you said I took after your cousin Mendela, who always thought he was upside down?"**

**"Oh, no," his father contemplated. "You must take after your mother's side, who they started from Poland to come to this country and wound up in Lithuania!"**

**"Were they lefty or righty?"**

**"Marvin, please...you're killing my *kishkas*..."**

**A shot rang out and Kopfelman woke and started running without looking back and with only the vaguest instinctive perception of going west, or going left—or not knowing where the hell he was going—but running his ass off to beat the band...the marching band way off in the distance whose faint refrain he now used as a compass-and-guide down street after street of ramshackle houses and winding lanes that seemed to have no end to them of twists and turns and inner regressions. All of it in a complex maze, a nightmare run from which there was no turning**

**back or sure way out, but Kopfelman sprinted harder and harder and followed the row of ramshackle houses until he had reached a clearing ahead of noise and lights, and blindly, desperately, stumbled across the finish line of the *Rua Visconde de Carvalas*… where he found himself back at the hospital.**

**He froze in amazement, leaning against a wall for support and gasping for breath, his mind awash with the giddy terrors of self-inspired lunacy and hallucination, though not denying the inescapable, upended hulk of the laundry truck that rested on the front lawn of the hospital like a disemboweled Mardi Gras float, surrounded by squad cars and curious bystanders poking each other as though there were something funny about it.**

**How had he gone in circles this way?**

**Was it possible he was even worse than his mother's family, by having gone from Poland—to Poland?**

**Kopfelman stood for a very long time as though paralyzed, then wandered about in a total daze, allowing himself to be passively jostled and dragged along to the other side of the boulevard before he felt his legs giving out and slithered along the plateglass window of an antique shop like a curled-up piece of dying confetti.**

**So this was the way it ended, he thought.**

**Not with a bang, but with cold concrete underneath his ass and people dropping coins at him.**

**All he needed was a cane and pencils…set up a little concession stand…get a seeing-eye dog…**

**"Are you all right?" Somebody shook his arm.**

**"Yes, the witch doctor said I should rest here a moment," Kopfelman grinned insensibly. "Can you give me a hand?"**

**He was given a hand and edged his way toward a coffee shop, sinking lower and lower with each stride he took and shlepping along with the bag in his hand like Groucho Marx.**

**"Do you rumba?"**

**"Yes."**

**"Then pick a rumba from one to ten."**

**"Kopfelman entered the coffee shop and asked the cashier for a cup of coffee.**

**"We don't got no coffee. We only got tea."**

**"All right, I'll have a cup of tea."**

**"I'm not the waitress."**

**"You look like an actress."**

**"We don't got that here."**

**"You got bialys?"**

**"I'm never hearing this word before."**

**"I'll have a roll."**

**"We don't got no rolls. We only got bread."**

**"Where are the phone booths?"**

**"Inside," she said.**

**He unzipped the bag and pulled out a hundred dollar bill.**

**"Just get me a piece of toast and butter."**

**He dialed the hotel and Josephine answered anxiously.**

**"Marvin?"**

"No, it's the FBI."

"What happened?"

"Look, I'm falling apart and I don't have time to explain right now, but they know who I am—or who I'm not—and I managed to get away from them."

"Where are you?"

"Would you believe this?" He laughed. "I'm across the street from the hospital, which is where I escaped from an hour ago when the world was young."

"You sound drunk or something."

"Punch-drunk, yes. I'm on a high of unknown dimensions."

"Just stay where you are."

"It's a coffee shop across the street from the hospital, but the main street here is completely blocked off to any traffic."

"I'll walk," she said. "The hotel is only a few blocks *west* of where you are."

"Look, please, don't give me directions, all right?"

"What's wrong with you?"

"I love you."

"That's what's wrong with you?"

"I'm not making sense."

"Don't panic," she said, "and just stay put."

"I couldn't move if I wanted to."

"I'll be right there."

He crept toward a table and watched the door, imagining all sorts of lurid scenarios, hoping that no one would get to him first

**before Josephine, when something seemed to give way in him like a Mayan veil. Some heightened sense of total awareness that all his life he'd been running from people, or waiting for people in coffee shops…like that stupid, ridiculous blind date he had in the luncheonette in Rego Park where he got his bialys, arranging to meet some woman there he had written to in the personal ads for desperate "Singles":** ***Wasp, Stunning, Scintillating, Seeks Renaissance Man*****…a woman who had consented to meet him, but then was annoyed and disappointed and making it known in every way that he wasn't who she thought he would be.**

**"Why, who were you expecting," he said, "Leonardo da Vinci?"**

**"I was frankly hoping for someone taller."**

**"I gave you my height on the telephone."**

**"Yes, I know," she said, "but sometimes these things are very misleading."**

**"How could five feet nine be very misleading?"**

**"I had no idea your hands were so small."**

**"My hands are small?"**

**"Oh, yes," she said.**

**"I never noticed," Kopfelman tried to minimize. "Do you find that offensive?"**

**"I find it very unmasculine."**

**"Well, no one is perfect," Kopfelman made his last appeal. "We all have our faults."**

**"I have nothing at all in common with you."**

"Oh, yes, you have," he reached across to her lovingly. "We both don't have any fucking tits!"

The things that were coming back to him.

The waitress came with an order of soup and garlic bread and dumped it down on a place mat that had stains on it.

"Enjoy your food, *con mucho gusto*."

"I believe I ordered come toast and tea."

"This is better for you."

"Oh, is it??"

"Si, *seguro*," she said. "You are looking too weak for a piece of toast."

Kopfelman looked for Tony Stabile to blow out his brains at any moment, and here he was in a coffee shop, without any coffee or toast or tea, getting unsolicited medical advice from the hired help while staring into a bowl of soup like an idiot.

"I like the way you do business here."

"You like some *Feijeada*?"

"No, don't even let it cross your mind."

"Is very good on Monday night."

"This is Sunday night."

"We have all the days for every night."

"Just do me a favor and call me if somebody finds my order."

"No water, no, we no drink the water. We only boil."

"Do you understand what I'm saying to you?"

"Oh, yes," she smiled beatifically. "The Mardi Gras is so beautiful, yes—is *fantastico*."

**The fantastic part was that Kopfelman felt a rising sense of euphoria at the thought of his not being understood, or maybe it was the fatigue he was feeling, the giddy notion and general air of goofiness that anything anyone said or did had absolutely no meaning at all, and that even the men who pursued him now with such deadly vengeance were just as unreal as his not having ordered the garlic bread, or his waiting here to be rescued from them by Josephine.**

**"Marvin."**

**Josephine rushed through the shop (in a dark velour outfit and bolo hat) and waited until the waitress had left before she would say another word.**

**"You look terrible."**

**"Thanks."**

**"Your face is green."**

**"I've been running in circles all night long."**

**"Are you sure you weren't followed here?"**

**"I lost them, but they must be out there looking for me."**

**He opened the bag to show her what they were looking for, but Josephine only noticed the gun he had stashed inside."**

**"Are you thinking of going to Catholic school."**

**"I got it the hard way."**

**"Then take my advice and get rid of it the easy way before you end up killing yourself."**

**"It saved me."**

**"How?"**

**"It scared people off."**

**"Did you notice that the catch was on?"**

**"The catch of what?"**

**"The safety catch!" She slipped the gun inside her purse. "I hate like hell to sit here and say I told you so."**

**"Don't say a word, you look beautiful.**

**"Yeah?" She was still incensed. She considered how he had talked her into disregarding her own finer instincts for basic survival, and reached out and pinned his hand in hers. "I've been worried sick."**

**"You think my hands are too small for me?"**

**"I think your head is too small for you!"**

**"Here, try a little garlic bread. It only costs a hundred dollars."**

**"What the hell are you talking about??"**

**"I've been hearing voices all night long."**

**"What kind of voices?"**

**"Lines from movies, all kinds of crazy mixed-up stuff from somewhere in my background, I guess…"**

**"Your parents?"**

**"I don't know," he said, "but one of them sounds like Ethel Merman."**

**"Don't feel so bad. We can always use a singer in the family."**

**"Well, this one sings with a vacuum cleaner."**

**"Sounds like it might be your mother," she said.**

**"A nice, loving family."**

**"Not any more than mine is, darling."**

**"Kopfelman noticed that two old ladies were staring at them and lowered his voice.**

**"Speaking of families…Mission accomplished. The fat man is dead."**

**"Marvin!" Josephine crossed her arms and held herself. "You've done it," she cried. "You've managed to do the impossible."**

**"The impossible I could always do," he shrugged at her, "it's the ordinary that fucks me up."**

**"Well, fucked up or not, my father is deeply indebted to you."**

**"For your hand in marriage?"**

**"For more than that."**

**"I'll settle for home sweet home with you."**

**"If we live that long."**

**"That's exactly what I'm thinking about. I have to make that flight to New York."**

**"Are you having some sort of breakdown or something?"**

**What do you mean?"**

**"That's the first place they'll be looking for you."**

**"Then there has to be an alternative plan."**

**"I'll give you an alternative plan," she rapped him one. "The important thing is to get you back to my hotel alive, and then we can talk of alternatives."**

**"Excuse me..." It was one of the women across the way who'd been staring at them. "But aren't you Marvin Kopfelman?"**

**Josephine reached inside her purse and deftly removed the safety catch on Rinzi's gun. She had seen too many benign old ladies in black shawls and mourning setting up someone and blowing away the best of them while thumbing through a bag of potatoes.**

**Kopfelman gaped in bewilderment.**

**"How is it that you know my name?"**

**"You mean to say you don't recognize me?"**

**"No, who are you?"**

**"I'm a colleague of yours. We've been searching all over the place for you. We thought you were dead."**

**"I was mugged," he explained. "I have no recollection of who I am."**

**"Amnesia!" Mrs. Covington gasped. "I knew it had to be something like that." She signaled over to the other table. "Yetta, dear, it's him, all right."**

**"I thought so," Mrs. Epstein cried. We've been to the embassy, local police."**

**"Ida's been absolutely frantic," Mrs. Covington rolled her eyes. "You do remember Ida Blavatnik?"**

**"Who's Ida Blavatnik?" Josephine tucked her purse away.**

**"She's tour guide for the United Federation of Teacher's Art Convention. Ida's the one who's responsible for our entire trip at**

**cut-rate fares and twenty percent off all hotel accommodations, including meals."**

**"I seem to remember something about her, Kopfelman strained.**

**"You have no idea who you are at all?" Mrs. Epstein yelped.**

**"Whatever you say will be news to me."**

**So they gave him the news in non-stop fashion, pausing every now and then to gather the impact on Josephine.**

**"I can't believe I teach in a high school."**

**"All of us feel the same way, dear," Mrs. Covington smiled. "You've been teaching there over twenty years and living at home with your lovely parents."**

**"You know them?"**

**"No, not really," she said, "but, unfortunately, we had to inform them immediately the moment you were 'missing in action', so to speak."**

**Kopfelman grew more depressed by the moment.**

**"How did they react to all this?"**

**"Well, your father said you were probably lost, and your mother wanted to know the terms of insurance coverage in case something terrible happened to you."**

**"Does any of this sound familiar?" Mrs. Epstein asked.**

**"Yes, things are beginning to stir up a bit."**

**"Your face looks green."**

**"It's incredible," Mrs. Covington interrupted at once, "how we met this way so fortuitously. Our hotel is right across the**

**street from the medical center. We come here for soup and garlic bread almost every night."**

**"I think it's the only thing they serve."**

**"Oh, no," she said, "we just finished having toast and tea."**

**They got his order, the sonofabitches.**

**"When, exactly, does your tour end?" Josephine intervened.**

**"That's exactly what I was getting at. We were due to leave this afternoon, but they called to tell us the plane was leaking—as though it were some sort of urinary problem, and booked us at this ridiculous hour."**

**"This Mardi Gras madness begins to wear thin after several days," Mrs. Epstein clucked. "It's a jungle out there with all this Mumbo-Jumbo business."**

**"What time does your flight depart?"**

**"At ten o'clock, but they always want you there early, you know, just to wait around. The driver of the jitney bus that leaves for the airport is sitting up front at the counter there. The bus is across the street right now."**

**"Are you coming with us?" Mrs. Covington placed a very assuring, maternal hand on Kopfelman's arm while accidentally resting her foot on Josephine's toe. "I don't know about your lady friend, but you do have a seat on the charter flight."**

**"Well, to tell you the truth…"**

**"Could we please have some time to discuss this matter?" Josephine disengaged her toe and rose politely to thank them both. "I'm sure you can appreciate the delicacy of our situation."**

**"Well, of course, if there's any problem involved..." Mrs. Covington blinked imperiously.**

**"If you don't mind, please."**

**The ladies retreated to pay their check. "We'll inform the others."**

**"Yes, do so, we'll be out in a moment."**

**Josephine couldn't believe their luck.**

**"What's this truth you were going to tell them about?"**

**"I sort of thought we'd go back together."**

**"This is better, safer, what's wrong with you?"**

**"I feel all confused."**

**"There's nothing to be confused about. You wanted an alternative plan? Well, God just sent down two *cacchiaroni* to lead the way. Who can ask for a better front than that to lead interference?"**

**"What's *cock-your-own-ee*?" Kopfelman asked.**

**"What your mother does when she's not collecting insurance money."**

**"They must have said I was dead or something."**

**"Don't even bother thinking about it, just go back with them and..." Josephine pressed her hands to her mouth. "Oh, Jesus Christ—*the money*!"**

**"What?"**

**"You no longer have the fat man's connections to get through customs."**

Kopfelman had to think hard about it, but Josephine couldn't forgive herself for the oversight.

"How could I overlook such a thing?"

"Don't feel so bad."

"You got me so crazy, I don't know what I'm doing anymore."

"I seem to have that effect on people."

"You trust me?"

"No, I'm waiting here for the bus to Boston."

"Listen," she said, "this will really be a test of what we mean to each other. Give me the money, I'll give it to Carmine, and Carmine will use his own connections to get it through customs."

"You trust him?"

"No, but we don't seem to have much choice in the matter. I'll contact you as soon as I book a flight out of here."

"You don't even know where I live," he said, "and neither do I."

"I'll find you, darling, don't worry about it."

But what if something should happen to her and she didn't call, or couldn't call—like when Deborah Kerr and Cary Grant were supposed to meet on New Year's Eve (at the top of the Empire State Building, yet!) as proof that they really loved each other, and Deborah gets hit by a taxicab while crossing the street, and Cary thinks she's rejecting him by not showing up, and that maybe she never loved him at all.

"Is there anything wrong?"

"I was thinking," he said, "that…"

**"What?" She said. "You look very upset."**

**His entire life was a blank to him, yet he still remembered these stupid movies and every nagging dumb cliché that passed through his mind with the cunning of Existential Dread.**

**"I was thinking that maybe if something goes wrong, I should have some way of contacting you."**

**"The Matarazza Funeral Home. I'm there all the time. I thought you knew."**

**"No, you never told me your father ran a funeral home."**

**"It's a front," she grinned. "I'll tell you about it some other time when this whole thing is over." She wiped away some smutch from his face. "We" have to go into deep hibernation. All skeletons in the closet exposed. If that doesn't send you running for the hills, then nothing will."**

**"You're the only thing that makes sense to me."**

**"Will you put that in writing?"**

**"I'm serious."**

**"Yes, and so am I."**

**He gave her the bag, and Josephine gave up her lips to him in a last embrace that had everything in it but background music.**

**"Just do me a favor and walk me across the street to the bus. I don't want to face that crowd alone."**

**"Whatever made you become a teacher?"**

**"I don't know," he said. "It must have been a recessive gene."**

∞∞

## 15

**On the bus, there was a grand reunion. People he didn't recognize and had never ever seen before were hugging and embracing him, and asking him all the obvious questions that Mrs. Epstein was kind enough to answer for him.**

**"He went for a walk after Reichbach gave that boring speech, so they mugged him, took his wallet and money, and that's what happens in a country that acts like *vilde chayas* when it comes to dancing, yet fails to produce not even the slightest inclination toward economic and social reform."**

**"Yetta, please, we don't need a Marxist interpretation to explain amnesia." Ida Blavatnik moved from the rear of the crowded bus and made her way toward Kopfelman. She was short and squat and efficient looking. She also wore orthopedic shoes and reminded him of a fire hydrant that no one had ever tried to turn on, or screw back in place, not even in the summertime. "I don't know if you remember me. We spent many pleasant evenings together." Her words were directed at**

**Josephine, who in turn glanced back at Kopfelman in disbelief. "Surely, there must be some recognition?"**

**Kopfelman's mouth dried up on him in embarrassment. He could not, for the life on him, imagine spending an evening with her unless he were having surgery done.**

**"It's hard to recognize anyone now," he shrugged in discomfort. "You just don't look familiar to me."**

**"I'll say she don't!" A heavyset man in bush jacket and Safari hat weaved drunkardly toward Kopfelman. "I suppose you don't remember me, either? Schneider the Schnorrer!"**

**Ida nudged him back a step.**

**"Will you please sit down?"**

**"I'm sorry, Ida, no harm intended. I didn't mean to stop you from being a pain in the ass."**

**"You're drunk again."**

**"That's the one part of this fucking tour you can't direct."**

**Mrs. Epstein reprimanded him and Ida pretended he didn't exist.**

**"There's one in every crowd," she smiled, "but I want you to know," she redirected her sensual wares back at Kopfelman, "we were all upset and concerned about you. I mean, no one in the entire history of the United Federation of Teachers has ever been lost or disappeared on a tour before. It was just the furthest thing from our mind, and nobody knew what had happened to you."**

**"We know what happened," Schneider bellowed. "Just take a look at the lady he's with."**

**All the men in the bus took their cue from this and were cheering, whistling, and stamping their feet, when suddenly all the windows shattered from everywhere in a halo of bullets, and Josephine half-karated Kopfelman down to the floor amidst shrieking pandemonium.**

**"It's terrorists," Mrs. Epstein cried. "They must know I'm from Israel!"**

**Josephine crawled up front to the driver.**

**"Step on it, what are you waiting for?"**

**"I think I'm...bleeding."**

**"Take my hand." She helped ease him down and slid behind the wheel of the bus. "Hold on everybody!"**

**She kicked off into a screaming turn and took part of another car with her as she tried shaking loose from the lane she was in, and jumped the divider, speeding upstream against startled hordes of oncoming traffic.**

**"You're going in the wrong direction." Ida stepped over Kopfelman's head. "You'll get us killed."**

**"Get down, you fool."**

**But Ida gave her the fullback plunge and grabbed the wheel.**

**"You're not the driver. *I'm* in charge."**

**The bus careened from side to side and was on the verge of a head-on collision, when Mrs. Covington body-slammed Ida down to the floor and punched her in the tits and stomach.**

**"Don't say another word, you bitch, or I'll sit on your face!"**

**"Go see if anyone else is hurt beside the driver," Josephine yelled back at Kopfelman.**

**He crawled and squeezed through the narrow aisle on his hands and knees and almost bumped heads with a bald-headed lady, groping for something beneath her seat.**

**"Did you lose something?"**

**"Yes, I lost my wig...and all my goddamn luggage is ruined, all the souvenirs I bought for my family."**

**Ida responded angrily under Mrs. Covington's two-armed pin.**

**"I want you to know we're insured for this, but I don't know about unlicensed drivers."**

**"Somebody's having trouble breathing," someone shouted. "I think it's Mr. Muhlenberg."**

**"Then why is he smoking?"**

**"Why are there people shooting at us and chasing us?"**

**"That's what I'd like to know!" A black woman answered indignantly. "I mean, all we did was take a few extra hotel towels."**

**"In Argentina, you *disappear*," Mrs. Epstein croaked.**

**Schneider the Schnorrer slumped to the floor by Kopfelman and offered him a swig of vodka.**

**"Marvin, you got some kind of woman. Where did she learn to drive like that?"**

**"In Catholic school."**

**"If I ever get out of this thing alive, I'm sending all my fucking kids there."**

**Josephine swerved and swung back over the road divider, hurtling into a sickening slide in the right direction.**

**"Watch out for the truck!"**

**She fishtailed into a hairpin turn that suddenly leaped out away from them into harrowing close-ups of nothingness, then reared back into focus again through the underbelly of slums and side streets, weaving a web so complexly wrought that Kopfelman sensed he was doomed to go in circles forever.**

**"Where are we going?"**

**"You wanted to go on a bus trip with the woman you loved? Well, now you know what it's all about!"**

**"This is not exactly what I had in mind."**

**"When it comes to your mind, let's not talk about it."**

**"You're angry."**

**"No, the glass in my hair is for decoration."**

**"You're bleeding!"**

**"That's from your girlfriend there. She scratched my face."**

**"She's not my girlfriend."**

**"All right, Marvin, let's not argue."**

**"I knew I shouldn't have come back here."**

**"Will you stop complaining and look to see if we're losing them?"**

**"I don't see any cars behind us," Kopfelman strained, "but I think we're getting lost ourselves."**

"I never get lost," she zinged at him. "We can't be very far from the airport."

"How do you know that?"

"I just keep in mind that we're going north."

"But how can you tell where north is from here?"

"It's parallel to the road we were on."

"*Parallel*?" He repeated, as though she had uttered the magic word that would now put him in complete possession of everything from the Missing Link to the Word Made Flesh. "With all these crazy twists and turns, we're still parallel to the same road that you crossed before to go against traffic in the wrong direction, before heading back in the right direction?"

"It's really not that complicated."

"I must be dyslexic."

"You'll be all right."

"We'll end up in Lithuania, yet…"

"We'll end up in a garbage heap if we run out of gas."

"We're out of gas?"

"They must have hit the fuel line or something. We're practically down to nothing here."

Kopfelman braced an arm about her, bowing his head on the guardrail by the driver's seat in genuflection.

"What're you doing?" Josephine asked.

"I'm praying."

"Good."

"Should I also make the sign of the cross?"

**"No, just make sure you hang on tight. We're going for broke!"**

**She zoomed off down the labyrinth of alleys and twisting side streets until she had reached the outer limits of the maze they were in, then burst out into the open again, honking, veering, bulling her way down the still congested thoroughfare to the overhead loop of a transverse highway, all signs pointing north of them to the entrance ramp of *Aeroporte Internationale*, and everyone shouting and cheering wildly—but much too soon—for a hospital van appeared out of nowhere and opened fire.**

**"It's them again!" Mrs. Epstein screamed. The windshield shattered and Josephine ducked momentarily with Kopfelman climbing on top of her to steady the wheel.**

**"You got it?"**

**"Yes, I got it!" She screamed. "Will you give them the goddamn money back before we get killed? That's all they're after."**

**"Sure," he said. "Just stop the bus and I'll get out and put a target on my head and make the exchange."**

**"Will you please unzip the bag for me?"**

**He opened the bag and Josephine tore out a fistful of money and flung it out of the open window, watching it flutter upward and outward in swirling motes of deflected light as everyone stared aghast at her.**

**"Now dump out all the rest of it."**

**"You mean, everything?"**

**"Yes."**

**"No souvenirs?"**

**"Nothing."**

**"Not even carfare?"**

**"Get rid of it now and stop all the stalling."**

**"*You crazy cunt*!" They cursed at her from the hospital van. "*You're throwing your fucking life away…*"**

**"You hear what they're saying?"**

**"Forget what they're saying and listen to me," she finally choked. "We're running out of goddamn gas!"**

**Kopfelman gave a long, last look at the desolate money, heard someone crying out to him: "It doesn't pay to be rich when you're dead," then held the bag by the open window and let it all suction out at them, and at all the cars in back of them—and immediately there was a chain reaction the likes of which he had never ever seen before.**

**"Did they go for it?"**

**"No, they're braking for animals," Kopfelman shouted.**

**"Oh, my God!" Mrs. Epstein moaned. "There are people smashing into each other."**

**"I think there must be a ten-car collision," Schneider called out ecstatically.**

**Kopfelman stuck his head out the window and sadly reviewed the last of the money flickering down in the eerie glow of wall-to-wall cars and twisted headlights.**

**"Does anyone know a Yiddish expression for *Ah-fongoo*?"**

**"The cops are coming!" Somebody shouted.**

**"*Oy Gevalt*!" Mrs. Epstein cried.**

**"*Finalmente…*" Josephine sighed to herself and eased off onto the entrance ramp of *Aeroporte Internationale* as sirens blared and everyone searched the floor for money.**

ꝏꝏ

# 16

As luck would have it (and luck had finally prevailed for them as the "X" factor even Kopfelman's unknown variables and lack of direction could not destroy), Ida Blavatnik was treated for shock and hospitalized, and Josephine readily took her place on the flight back home as the other woman.

"I never thought we'd make it," she said, as they boarded the plane, awaiting takeoff. "She's the best thing that ever happened to us."

"Who, Ida?"

"Yes."

"She has what is known as instinctive *chutzpa*," Kopfelman added, "which isn't all that bad, I guess, when you're suing two hundred million people."

Ida was suing the UFT, the teacher's convention, the charter flight company, Mrs. Covington (for assault and battery), and also the entire Brazilian government for not providing adequate protection while visiting as a guest in their country.

**"She'll probably make the late night news with intravenous tubes up her ass and a State of the Union message for teachers all over the world."**

**Josephine wasn't about to complain.**

**"I hope you're not disappointed," she said, "about having to part with all that money."**

**"Parting with that much pasta, darling, even when it's lowdown, dirty, tainted money, immorally conceived and gained—is like planting a bomb in your Super-Ego."**

**"We'll help you put back the pieces," she said.**

**"The pieces, sure..." He rubbed along the wall of his jaw and swallowed his voice like Marlon Brando. "I could'da been a contender, Charlie. Now all I got is my pension plan."**

**"And me," she said.**

**"And you," he said. "You were really terrific. I love the way you handled yourself."**

**"I was terrible."**

**"What're you talking about?"**

**"I shouldn't have taken over that way."**

**"What way was that?"**

**"What I did before. I should have allowed you to act for yourself."**

**"I was acting."**

**"Yes, but I should have let you assume control and drive the bus."**

"Are you kidding me?" Kopfelman laughed at her. "If I drove the bus and assumed control, we would all be back at the hospital with Ida Blavatnik—or circling the globe."

But Josephine wouldn't put in with that.

"I'm so used to giving orders, Marvin, it's almost like second nature to me. I just take over without even having to think about it."

"Don't think about it, I like taking orders."

"You don't feel it's emasculating?"

Kopfelman smiled at her wistfully.

"You know that song I Left My Heart in San Francisco?"

"Tony Bennett."

"Yeah," he said. "Well, I left my balls in a laundry truck on the *Rua Visconde de Caravalas*, and I ain't ever going back for them, so not to worry," he comforted. "You were great back there, and not only am I proud of you, and in awe of you, but it's nice to know you can drive a bus in emergencies—in case we need any extra money."

"You lousy fink!"

They grabbed at each other, and Kopfelman felt an uplifting oceanic surge of everything they had been through together, as though he were finally at one with himself, while Josephine, who had all she could do to keep from bursting (for having held in her breath so long), expired along the contours of his chest like a wounded, surrealistic balloon.

**"Don't worry about the money," she said. "My father is deeply indebted to you, and don't think he's not going to pay for it when I break the news that we're getting married."**

**Kopfelman stirred uneasily.**

**"I thought you were declaring your independence from him??"**

**"Yes, *after* the wedding, but first I want what's coming to me."**

**"I'll probably have to invite my parents—whoever they are—just to be respectful."**

**"I have the feeling they're not as bad as you think they are."**

**"I have the feeling my mother will sing the national anthem."**

**"My mother will haunt me the rest of her life if I don't put on her wedding gown in keeping with our family tradition."**

**"You think it'll fit?"**

**"Well, my mother weighed over two hundred pounds, but not when she was married, of course."**

**"Are you giving me a message here?"**

**"You're getting a bargain, so stop complaining."**

**"Your father might be a bigger problem," Kopfelman added. "He probably has Jews embroidered all over the inside of his underwear."**

**"Oh, no," she demurred. "He always does what I want him to do, I can handle him, but Carmine...well, he's the older brother, and long ago we made it up he would be best man."**

**"I don't think your brother likes me too much."**

**"He doesn't really dislike you at all."**

**"He threatened to kill me."**

**"He didn't know who you were at the time."**

**"And now that he knows, we'll play chess together?"**

**"He might surprise you."**

**"No more surprises!"**

**"Okay," she said. "I'll lay it on the line for you. Expect to have a real Woppo wedding, the likes of which you have never ever seen before, withy plenty of money pouring in from every member, of every family, in the Organization."**

**"I believe in the family," Kopfelman nodded seriously, "as long as I don't have to live in a tent at the Matarazza Funeral Home."**

**"That's out," she said. "We're going to leave that far behind us and do all the things we planned to do."**

**"Legitimate?"**

**"Yes, the straight and narrow all the way. I'll find some work in fashion designing, and you'll do your teaching, and then we'll go on a long vacation to Europe somewhere, and start a little family of our own."**

**"You mean, little Josephine Kopfelmans?"**

**"And maybe a little Don Vincenzo."**

**"What about all the starving artists you wanted to save? The gallery down in Greenwich Village."**

**"The more they starve, the more they create. In the meantime, we'll go bourgeois awhile."**

**The sign went on to fasten seatbelts.**

**"Tired?"**

**"Yes, my eyes are starting to close on me," he apologized. "I hope I don't fall asleep on you."**

**"Don't worry about it. Sleep," she said.**

**The plane taxied neatly along the runway and then roared off into magical, mystical airdromed darkness, high above the departing lights of the coastal plain and all that they were leaving behind that would someday serve to energize both their past and future in ways she could not anticipate now, and that seemed to awaken some newly discovered sense of herself in which old betrayals and long-lost loves were no longer like sacrificial rites.**

**It was all set in her mind this way quite peacefully, in the randomness and growing abstraction of time and space, when she noticed that her seat was bouncing up and down and starting to shake like one of those vibrating motel beds that Josephine thought might possibly be an airlines gimmick for settling nerves, but which turned out to be a precipitous plunge into turbulence that unsettled all the overhead luggage, one of which bounced off Kopfelman's head and woke him at the very same time it dazed him momentarily.**

**"*Fasten your seatbelts*," a voice came over the intercom system.**

**"Thanks a lot," she yelled back as a stewardess rushed to give him aid.**

**"Are you all right, sir?"**

**"He'll be all right."**

**"He looks slightly dazed."**

**"Where am I?" Kopfelman rubbed his head.**

**"We're just going through a bumpy run. We're experiencing some sort of turbulence," the stewardess answered, referring herself back to Josephine. "Perhaps he's still in some sort of shock."**

**"I'll give you a shock," she grabbed at him. "Marvin, what you are talking about? We're on the plane. We're going home..."**

**"He's not responding."**

**"Oh, Jesus Christ!"**

**"Has anything like this happened before?"**

**"I don't even want to think about it."**

**"I'll get him something to bring him around."**

**She was on the verge of asking for something to bring her around, but merely replaced the fallen luggage, which didn't even belong to them—and God forbid he should ever take an aisle seat again!**

**"Marvin, listen—look at me, damn it!"**

**Kopfelman followed the sound of her voice, but seemed to have trouble focusing.**

**"Sorry, madam...I'm not feeling well."**

**"What's this madam bullshit? This is me, this is Josephine! Don't you know who I am?"**

**He paused to get a closer look and peered intently.**

**"Josephine...that's an *Eye*-talian name..." His voice grew stiff and strangely British. "I don't believe we've ever had the pleasure of meeting."**

**"You're *Marvin*," she shook him savagely. "Your name is Marvin Kopfelman!"**

**"Oh, no," he warned deprecatingly. "I can well understand your being attracted to Jewish men, but you must be thinking of someone else who looks like me. My name is Ronald Coleman," he grinned—then quickly ducked to defend himself against everything and the kitchen sink that Josephine threatened to murder him with every day of their lives, until death did them part at *Random Harvest*.**

**"I was almost about to sue the airlines, you imbecile!"**

**"I knew I would end up with Ida Blavatnik," he zetzed her back.**

**"You should only live to be so lucky."**

**Kopfelman bowed in total surrender.**

**"Forgive me, darling, I couldn't resist."**

**"Oh, shut up with your British accent."**

**"Love me?"**

**"No!—and next time you pull a stunt like that, I'll name all the children *Nunzio*."**

**And two hours later, completely resigned to their craziness and possible lifetime of total irrationality, they ate and watched a grade "Z" movie...and Josephine gently removed his glasses as Kopfelman dozed and snored his way to the promised land.**

ꝏꝏ